William H. H. Murray

Mamelons and Ungava

a legend of the Saguenay

William H. H. Murray

Mamelons and Ungava
a legend of the Saguenay

ISBN/EAN: 9783337392284

Printed in Europe, USA, Canada, Australia, Japan

Cover: Foto ©Andreas Hilbeck / pixelio.de

More available books at **www.hansebooks.com**

MAMELONS AND UNGAVA

A Legend of the Saguenay.

[redacted]

[redacted]

[redacted]

To that American who knows and loves the Legendary Lore of his native land, and appreciates what I would fain do for it if I were able; who, distinguished by the brightness of his wit, the gentleness of his nature, and his love of polite letters, is beloved by all who know him; to

George Stewart, Jr., D.C.L., D. Litt., F.R.G.S.,

of Quebec, I inscribe this Tale of Mamelons.

The Author.

Burlington, Vt., 1890.

CONTENTS.

AUTHOR'S PREFACE.

I HAVE for some years felt that the connection of the old races with the North American Continent, the signs and proofs of whose presence are to be found almost everywhere, and nowhere so frequently as on the St. Lawrence, afforded material for entertaining authorship. Prompted by this feeling, I have, during these several years past, been working at certain pieces of composition, of which this bit of romance is a fair sample.

If it shall so far please the reading public that its publisher shall not lose money by his venture — for letters in our time have no patronage save from the hope of selfish gain — I shall, later on, print others like to it. But if it fail, as it quite likely will, to bring him commercial profit, then they will be forgotten as this one will, until I better them, or they come to a better time.

W. H. H. MURRAY.

BURLINGTON, VT., Jan. 7, 1887.

INTRODUCTION.

MY publishers have requested me to prepare a brief statement concerning my literary work, especially that portion of it relating to the character known as John Norton the Trapper—and the stories called the "Adirondack Tales." They represent that there is an unusual curiosity and interest on the part of many touching this matter, and that a brief statement from me, as the author of them, will please many and interest all who read my works.

I know that many thousands of people do feel in this way, for my mails for several years have brought me almost daily a most agreeable correspondence concerning not only the character of John Norton the Trapper, but the general scope and characteristics of my literary work; and because of this personal knowledge I do the more cheerfully comply with my publishers' request, and will, now and here, set down as briefly as I may what seems likely to be of interest to those who read this volume.

The first volume ever published, of my writing, was by the house of Ticknor & Fields, in 1868, I think, and had for its title "Murray's Adventures in the Wilderness." This was the book which first brought the Adirondacks to popular notice, and did so much to advertise that now famous region to the sporting and touring classes of the country. The noticeable thing as to this volume is that it was not prepared by me for publication, and while writing the several chapters I had no idea that they, or anything I should ever write, would be published. I was then in the clerical profession, and was stationed at Meriden, Conn. I had at this time a habit of composing each day, when my duties permitted me the leisure, some bits of writing wholly apart from my profession and work. They were of the nature of exercises in English composition, and had no other interest to me than the mental refreshment it gave me to write them, and the hope that the doing of them would assist me to improve my style in expression. They were constructed slowly and rewritten many times, until they were as simple and accurate as to the use of words as I could make them. I enjoyed the work very much, and the composition of those little bits of description and humor delighted me probably more than they ever have the readers of them. By an accident of circumstances they were printed in the *Meriden Recorder*, and, beyond pleasing a few hundreds of local readers, made no reputation for themselves whatever. At least, I never heard of them or gave them any thought. It was owing to James T. Fields that their merit, such as they had, was discovered, and that they were given in volume form to the world. Of the reception the little book met with at the hands of the public, I need not speak. As to it I know no one was more surprised than I was. It made the Adirondacks famous, and gave me a *nom de plume* which has almost overshadowed the name I was christened with. What pleases me most as to it is the thought that it helped to introduce healthier fashions of recreation, and brought thousands into close and happy connection with Nature.

Of several volumes of sermons that were published while I was in the clerical profession I make no mention, for I do not regard them as literary productions. They represent only a temporary popular demand, and as compositions only the low average possible to an overworked man, compelled by his duties to do too much to do anything well.

The volume known as the "Perfect Horse" was, I believe, with the exception of Hiram Woodruff's little volume, the first attempt made by an American author to teach the breeders of the trotting horse in this country the true principles and correct methods of equine propagation. It had a large sale, and, I have reason to think, helped the country to needed knowledge. To me it only stood for years of wide and close studentship of the question, and a benevolent endeavor.

The prompting motive in the preparation of "Daylight Land" was this: The little book "Adventures in the Wilderness" was published in 1868, I think, and under circumstances such as I have explained. I had no thought at that time of becoming an author. The several chapters of that little volume were written as exercises in composition. I was, at the writing of them, only some twenty-six years old. I knew little of life or nature, and absolutely nothing of what literary balance and fitness mean. My knowledge of woodcraft was then slight, of the American Continent slighter yet. Naturally the book, because of the fame it won, became, as years passed, my knowledge grew apace, and my power of expression ripened, a regret to me. It did not in any sense represent me as an author. This feeling was shared by others who have regard for my writings, especially along the lines of description and entertainment; and I was urged to compose a volume of the same general character as my first little book, that should be a fairer and happier expression of myself as an author, in the lighter moods of composition. It may interest some to learn — especially young authors and literary folk — that "Daylight Land" had for its prompting cause the feeling that it was not fit for me to be permanently represented in descriptive writing and in composition of the lighter sort, by that little book that has gone so far and done so much of good in many ways, but which, because of the reasons stated, has always been extremely unsatisfactory to me.

I will now come directly to the character of John Norton the Trapper and the "Adirondack Tales."

I was once at a luncheon at which Mr. James T. Fields presided. Several clever literary men of more or less prominence were present. Mr. Emerson was there, and in answer to the query, "What makes a story a great story," said: "A story which will make the average reader laugh and cry both is a great story, and he who writes it is a true author." The definition struck me, when I heard it, as a very proper one; and it has influenced me in my choice of subjects and methods of treatment ever since.

Another question discussed at that table was this: "Why must the feminine element be introduced so constantly?" or, as one of the witty lunchers phrased it, "Why must every author forever introduce a woman into his story?"

This was discussed at length, all assuming that such necessity did exist.

I had not engaged in the spirited talk, being well content to listen. This Mr. Fields noted, and insisted on "Parson Murray"—as he facetiously called me—giving his views. I replied that I would sooner keep quiet, especially as I did not agree with the verdict of the table. This attracted a surprised attention, and I was compelled to say "that I did not see the need of introducing a woman into every story, and that I believed a story meeting Mr. Emerson's definition of a great story, viz., one which would make the readers of it laugh and cry both, could be written without a woman appearing in it, and that in some masculine natures was a tenderness as deep, a sympathy as sweet, and a love as strong as existed in woman." And I added, "Mr. Emerson has forgotten that in a book with which, as he was a clergyman for years, he is perfectly familiar, there is a picture given of two men who 'loved each other beyond the love of women.'"

Not to dilate further, from that day Mr. Fields never ceased to urge me to "attempt that story," and, being most friendly to me,— and to what young person with any talent was he not ever a friend?—he would say, "I tell you, Murray, try and see if you can write that story, not a woman or the hint of one, good or bad, in it; for it may be you might succeed, and if you should, you know what Emerson said; and I would like to be the publisher." Prompted by this kindly thought for me, and moved by assisting circumstances, I wrote the "Story of the Man Who Didn't Know Much." It was composed amid the pressure of journalistic as well as clerical labors, by being dictated to a type-writer, and appeared in the weekly issues of the *Golden Rule*, a journal of which I was editor and owner. It gave great satisfaction to the readers of the paper, and increased its circulation appreciably. Of its literary merit, if it had any, the readers of the volume can judge. The pleasantest thought to me, perhaps, concerning it, was the fact that Mr. Fields came one day to my study, and in his genial, earnest way exclaimed, "Murray, you have done what you said could be done; you have written a story up to the level of Emerson's definition, for I have read it from beginning to end, and laughed and cried over it both." It is doubtless owing to this story and the success of it, more than to any other cause, that my mind was turned toward literature as the field in which I could work with the greatest pleasure to myself, and perhaps with the largest resultant benefit to mankind. The character of the Lad was sketched with the desire to illustrate the beauty and moral force of innocence and simplicity, as contrasted with great mental endowments. It was from listening to the playing of the greatest master of the violin in modern times, Ole Bull, that I conceived the description of the Lad's violin and his manner of playing it at the ball. The great violinist expressed to me the delight the reading of the passage gave him, and jokingly declared that he enjoyed it all the more because it was composed by a man who couldn't play a note himself!

Of John Norton — and this must stand as answer to all the interrogations that have been put to me concerning him — I have this to say. I never saw any such man as John Norton; never saw one so good as he is, in my vision of him; never saw one who even suggested him. He is a creation, pure and simple, of my imagination. But, though I never saw such a man, he nevertheless stands for an actual type. Big-bodied, big-headed, big-hearted, wise, humorous, humane, brave, he types to me the old-fashioned New England man, who, having lived his life in the woods, has had developed in him those virtues and qualities of head and heart, of mind and soul, in harmony with his life-long surroundings. Through him, as my mouth-piece, I tell whatever of knowledge I have of woodcraft, whatever appreciation I have of Nature, and whatever wisdom I may have been taught by my communings with her silence. This is all I know of John Norton the Trapper. The "Story that the Keg told me" was composed simply to introduce the character of John Norton to the reader, to present him, as it were, to the reader's eye, and prepare him to appreciate his characteristics.

The "Adirondack Tales," as outlined in my mind, consist of six volumes, three of which are already written and await publication, the other three I hope to complete within the next five or six years. The Canadian Idyls will consist also of six volumes, the "Doom of Mamelons," "Ungava," and "Mistassinni" being the first three. In them I treat of the myths and traditions of the aboriginal races of America as located especially in the northern section of the continent, and they represent my best effort. It is not likely that much, if indeed any part, of what I may write will be granted a permanent place in the literature of my country, nor am I stirred to effort by any ambition or dream that it may. I shall be well satisfied if, by what I write, some present entertainment be afforded the reader: a love of nature inculcated; and encouragement given to a more manly or womanly life. As my expectation is modest, I am the more likely, perhaps, to live long enough to see some small part of it, at least, realized.

W. H. H. MURRAY.

BURLINGTON, VT.

ARGUMENT.

THE development of the story turns upon the working of an old Indian prophecy or tradition, which had been in the Lenni-Lenape tribe, to the effect, that when an intermarriage between a princess of their tribe and a white man should occur, it would bring ruin to the tribe, and cause it to become extinct at Mamelons. For it was at the mouth of the Saguenay, as they held, that the whites first landed on this western continent. This intermarriage, or "cross of red with white," had occurred, and the time had nearly come when the last of the race should, in accordance with the old prophecy, die at Mamelons.

The persons introduced into this tale are John Norton, the Trapper, who is comrade and bosom friend of the chief of the Lenni-Lenape; the chief himself, who is dying from an old wound received in a fight at Mamelons, and has sent a runner to summon the Trapper to his bedside, to receive his dying message; a very beautiful woman of that most peculiar and ancient of all known peoples, the Basques of Southern Spain, the last of their queenly line, who has been married in France by the chief's brother, and to whom a daughter has been born, Atla, the beautiful heroine of the story. And, in addition to these, is an old chief of the famous Mistassinni tribe, who had had his tongue cut out at the torture stake by the Esquimaux, from whose fury he had been rescued by a party of warriors, headed by the Trapper.

At Mamelons in a great fight, fought in the darkness and terror of an earthquake commotion, the chief of the Lenni-Lenape had, unknowingly, slain his brother, who, returning from France with his young Basque wife, had been wrecked on the coast of Labrador, and, out of gratitude to the Esquimaux, who had treated him kindly, he joined their ranks as they marched up to Mamelons to the great battle. Thus, fighting as foes, unknown to each other, in the darkness that enveloped the field, he was killed by his brother, having seriously wounded him in return.

The Basque princess, thus widowed by the

untimely death of her young husband, gave birth to Atla, who was thus born an orphan, and under doom herself. Her mother, soon after the birth of Atla, was rescued from death by the Trapper, and loved him with all the ardor of her fervent nature. His affections she strove and hoped to win, and would, perhaps, have succeeded, had not death claimed her. Dying, she left her love and hopes as an heritage to her daughter, and charged her, with solemn tenderness, to win the Trapper's affection, and, married to him, become the mother of a mighty race, in whose blood the beauty and strength of the two oldest and handsomest races of the earth should be happily mingled.

The chief, knowing of her wish, and the instructions left to Atla by her departed mother, summons the Trapper to his death-bed, to tell him the origin of the doom, and the possibility or surety of its being avoided by his loving and marrying Atla. For, by the conditions of the old curse it was proclaimed when spoken, that the "doom shall not hold in case of son born in the female line from sire without a cross," viz.:—from a pure-blooded white man. The Trapper in his humility feels himself to be unworthy of so splendid an alliance, and resists the natural promptings of his heart.

But at last the beautiful Atla wins him to a full confession; and at her urgent request, against the Trapper's wish, they start for Mamelons to be married, where, before the rite is concluded, she dies, so fulfilling the old prediction of her father's tribe.

In the Basque princess, the mother of Atla, the author has striven to portray an utterly unconventional woman, natural, barbaric, original; splendid in her beauty, and glorious in her passions, such as actually lived in the world in the far past, when women were—it must be confessed—totally unlike the prevalent type of to-day. In her child, Atla, the same type of natural womanhood is preserved, but slightly sobered in tone and shade of expression. But as studies of the beautiful and the unconventional in womanhood, both are unique and delightful.

NOTE.—The notes which have been connected in explanation of certain passages of the story, are so peculiarly interesting and suggestive that they make the reader wish that the author had extended them in fuller exposition of that "lore of woods and waters and of antique days" with which he is so familiar.

PUBLISHERS.

MAMELONS.[1]

A LEGEND OF THE SAGUENAY.

CHAPTER I.

THE TRAIL.

IT was a long and lonely trail, the southern end of which John Norton struck in answer to the summons which a tired runner brought him from the north. The man had made brave running, for when he reached the Trapper's cabin and had placed the birch-bark packet in his hands, he staggered to a pile of skins

[1] Mamelons. The Indians' name for the mouth of the Saguenay, and signifies the Place of the Great Mounds. See note 12.

and dropped heavily on them, like a hound which, from a three-days' chase, trails weakly to the hunter's door, spent nigh to death. So came the runner, running from the north, and so, spent with his mighty race, dropped as one dead upon the pile of skins.

He bore the death-call of a friend, whose friendship had been tested on many an ambushed trail and the sharp edge of dubious battle. The call was writ on bark of birch, thin as the thinnest silk the ancients wove from gossamer in the old days when weaving was an art and mystery, and not a sordid trade to earn a pittance with, traced in delicate letters by a hand the Trapper would have died for. A good five hundred miles that trail ran northward before it ended at the couch of skins, in the great room of the great house, in which the chief lay dying. And when the Trapper struck it he struck it as an eagle strikes homeward toward the cradle crag of his younglings, when talons are heavy and daylight scant. He drew his line by the star that never sets, and little turning did he make for rivers, rapids, or tangled swamp; for mountain slope or briery windfall. He drew a trail no man had ever trod — a blazeless[1] trail, unmarked by stroke

[1] In order to mark the direction of his course in trailing through the woods the trailer slashes with his axe or knife the bark of the trees he passes, by which signs he is able to retrace his course safely, or follow the same trail easily some future time. A blazed trail is one thus plainly marked. A blazeless trail is one on which the trailer has no marks or "blazes" to run by, but draws his line by other and occult signs, which tell him in what direction he is going and which are known only by those initiated in the mysteries of woodcraft.

of axe or cut of knife, by broken twig or sharpened rod, struck into mold or moss, and by its angle[1] telling whence came the trailer, whither went he, and how fast. From earliest dawn till night thickened the woods and massed the trees into a solid blackness, he hurried on, straight as a pigeon flies when homing, studying no sign for guidance, leaving none to tell that he had come and gone. He was at middle prime of life, tough and pliant as an ashen bough grown on hill, seasoned in hall, sweated and strung by constant exercise for highest action, and now each mus-

[1] Certain tribes of Indians north of the St. Lawrence left accurate record of their rate of progress, and how far they had come, by the length and angle of the slanted sticks they drove here and there into the ground as they sped on. The Nasquapees were best known as practicing this habit.

cle and sinew of his superb and superbly conditioned frame was taut with tension of a strong desire — to reach the bedside of the dying chief before he died. For the message read: "Come to me quick, for I am alone with the terror of death. The chief is dying. At the pillar of white rock, on the lake, a canoe, with oars and paddle, will be waiting."

The Trapper was clad in buckskin from cap to moccasins. His tunic, belted tight and fringeless, was opened widely at the throat for freest breathing. A pack, small, but rounded with strained fullness, was at his back. His horn and pouch were knotted to his side. In tightened belt was knife, and, trailing muzzle down and held reversed, a double rifle. Stripped was the man for speed, as when balanced on the issue of the race hang life and death. As some great ship, caught by some sudden gale off Anticosti or Dead Man's Reef, and bare of sail, stripped to her spars, past battures hollow and hoarse-voiced as death and ghastly white, and through the damned eddies that would suck her down and crush her with stones which grind forever and never see the light, sharpening their cuttings with their horrid grists, runs scudding; so ran the strong man northward, urged by a fear stronger than that of wreck on the ghost-peopled shore of deadly St. Lawrence. A hound, huge of size, bred to a hair, ambled steadily on at heel. And though he crossed many a hot scent, and more than once his hurrying master started a buck warm from his nest, and nose was busy with knowledge of game afoot, he gave no whimper nor swerved aside, but, silent, followed on in the swift way his master was so hurriedly making, as if he, too, felt the solemn need which urged the trail northward. Never before had runner faced a longer or a harder trail, or under high command or deadly peril pushed it so fiercely forward.

Seven days the trail ran thus, and still the man, tireless of foot, hurried on, and the hound followed silently at heel. What a body was his! How its powers responded to the soul's summons! For on this seventh day of highest effort, taxing with heavy strain each muscle, bone, and joint to the utmost, days lengthened from earliest dawn to deepest gloaming, the strong man's face was fresh, his eye was bright, and he swung steadily onward, with long, swinging, easy-motioned gait, as if the prolonged and terrible effort he was making was but a morning's burst of speed for healthy exercise.

The climate favored him. October, with all its glorious colors, was on the woods, and the warm body of the air was charged through and through with cool atmospheric movements from the north. It was an air to race for one's life in. Soft to the lungs, but filled to its blue edge with oxygen and that mystic element men call ozone; the overflow of God's vitality spilled over the azure brim of heaven, whose volatile flavor fills the nose of him who breathes the air of mountains. Favored thus by rare conditions, the best that nature gives the trailer, the strong man raced onward through the ripe woods like an old-time runner running for the laurel crown and the applause of Greece.

It was nigh sunset of the seventh day, and the Trapper halted beside a spring, which bubbled coldly up from a cleft rock at the base of a cliff. He cast aside his hunting shirt, baring his body to the waist, and bathed himself in the cool water. He knelt to its mossy rim and sank his head slowly down into the refreshing depths, and held it there, that he might feel the delicious coolness run thrilling through his heated body. He cast his moccasins aside and bathed his feet, sore and hot from monstrous effort, sinking them knee deep in the cold flowage of the blessed spring. Then, refreshed, he stood upon the velvet bank, his mighty chest and back pink as a lady's palm, his strong feet glowing, his face aflush through its deep tan, while the wind dried him, and the golden leaves of the overhanging maples fell round him in showers.

Refreshed and strengthened, he reclothed himself, relaced his moccasins and tightened belt, but before he broke away he drew the sheet of birch-bark from his breast and read again the lines traced delicately thereon.

"Yes, I read aright," he muttered to himself; "the writing on the birch is plain as ivy on the oak, and it says: 'Come to me quick, for I am alone with the terror of death. The chief lies dying. At the pillar of white rock, on the lake, a canoe, with oars and paddle, will be waiting.'" And the Trapper thrust the writing back to its place above his heart and burst away down the decline that led to the lake at a run.

"I've bent the trail like a fool," he muttered, as he reached the bottom of the dip, "or the lake lies hereaway," and even as he spoke the waters of a lake, red with the red flame of the setting sun, gleamed like a field of fire through the maple-trees. The Trapper dashed a hand into the air with a gesture of delight, and burst away again at a lope through the russet bushes and golden leaves that lay like plucked plumage, ankle deep, upon the ground toward the lake, burning redly through the trees not fifty rods beyond. A moment brought him to the shore, bordered thick with cedar growths, and, breaking through the fragrant branches with a leap, he landed on a beach of silver sand, and lo! to the left, not a dozen rods away, washed by the red waves, stood the signal rock, fifty feet in height, and from water line to summit white as drifted snow.

"God be praised!" exclaimed the Trapper, and he lifted his cap reverently. "God be praised that I reckoned the course aright and ran the trail straight from end to end. For the woods be wide and long, and to have missed this lake would have been a sorry hap when one like her is alone with the dying. But where is the canoe that she said should be here, for sixty miles of water cannot be jumped like a brook or forded like a rapid, and the island lies nigh the western shore, and who may reach it afoot?" And he ran his eyes along the sand for signs to tell if boat or human foot had pressed it.

He searched the beach a mile around the bay, but not a sign of human presence could be found. Then nigh the signal rock he sat upon the sand, unloosed his pack, and from it took crust and meat, of which he ate, then fed the hound, sharing the scant supper with him equally. "It is the last morsel, Rover," said the Trapper to the dog as he fed him. "It is the last morsel in the pack, and you and I will breakfast lightly unless luck comes." The dog surely understood the master's saying, for he rolled his hungry eyes toward the pack as if he bitterly sensed the bitter prophecy; then — canine philosopher as he was — he curled himself amid some dried leaves contentedly, as if by extra sleep he would make good the lack of food.

"Thou art wiser than men!" exclaimed the Trapper, looking reflectively at his canine companion, now snoring in his warm russet bed. "Thou art wiser, my dog, than men, for they waste breath and time in bewailing their hard fortunes, but you make good the loss that pinches thee by holding fast and quickly to the nearest gain." And he gazed upon the sleeping hound with reflecting and admiring eyes.

Then slowly behind the western hills sank the red sun. The fervor faded from the water and the lake darkened. The winds died with the day. Gradually the farther shore retired from sight, and the distinguishing hills became blankly black. The upper air held on to the retreating light awhile, but finally surrendered the last trace, and night held all the world.

Amid the gathering gloom upon the beach the Trapper sat in counsel with his thoughts.

At length he rose, and with dry driftage within reach kindled a fire. By the light of it he cut some branches of nigh cedars, and with them made a bed upon the sand, then cast himself upon his fragrant couch. Twice he rose and listened. Twice renewed the fire with larger sticks. At last, tired nature failed the will. The toil of the long trail fell heavily on him. Slumber captured his senses and he slept the sleep of sheer exhaustion. But before he slept he muttered to himself:

"She said a canoe, with oars and paddle, should be here, and the canoe will come."

The hours passed on. The Dipper turned its circle in the northern sky, and stars rose and set. The warm shores felt the coolness of the night, and from the water's edge a soft mist flowed and floated in thin layers along the cooling sands. The logs of seasoned wood glowed with a steady warmth in the calm air. The fog turned yellow as it drifted above the burning brands, so that a halo crowned the ruddy heat. The night was at its middle watch, when the hound rose to his feet and questioned the lake with lifted nose, but his mouth gave no signal. If one was coming, it was the coming of a friend. Ten minutes passed, then he whined softly, and, walking to the water's edge, waited expectant; not long, for in a moment a canoe, moving silently, as if wind-blown, came floating toward the beach, and lodged upon it noiselessly, as bird on bough. And a girl, paddle in hand, stepped to his side, and, stooping, caressed his head, then moved toward the fire and stood above the sleeping man.

She gently stirred the brands until they flamed, and in the light thus made studied the strong face, bronzed with the tan of the woods, the face of one who never failed friend nor fought foe in vain, and who had come so far and swiftly in answer to her call. She was of that old race who lived in the morning of the world, when giants walked the earth[1] and the sons of God married the daughters of men.[2] And the old blood's love of strength was in her. She noted the power and symmetry of his mighty frame, which lay relaxed

[1] "There were giants in the earth in those days." — GEN. vi. 4.

[2] "The sons of God saw the daughters of men that they were fair; and they took them wives of all which they chose." — GEN. vi. 2.

from tension in the graceful attitude of sleep; the massive chest, broad as two common men's, which rose and fell to his deep breathing; the great, strongly corded neck, rooted to the vast trunk as some huge oak grown on a rounded hill. She noted, too, the large and shapely head, the thick, black hair, closely cropped, and the sleeper's face — where might woman find another like it? — lean of flesh, large featured, plain, but stamped with the seal of honesty, chiseled clean of surplus by noble abstinence, and bearing on its front the look of pride, of power and courage to face foe or fate. Thus the girl sat and watched him as he slept, stirring the brands softly that she might not lose sight of a face which was to her the face of a god — such god as the proudest woman of her race, in the old time might, with art or goodness, have won and wedded.

Dawn came at last. The blue above turned gray. The stars shortened their pointed fires and faded. The east kindled and flamed. Heat flowed westward like an essential oil hidden in the pores and channels of the air; while light, brightly clean and clear, ran round the horizons, revealing its own and the loveliness of the world.

Then woke the birds. Morning found a voice sweet as her face. A hermit thrush sent her soft, pure call from the damp depths of the dripping woods. A woodpecker signalled breakfast with his hammer so sturdily that all the elfin echoes of the hills merrily mimicked him. An eagle, hunting through the sky, at the height of a mile, dropped like a plummet into the lake, and, struggling upward from his perilous plunge, heavily weighted, lined his slow flight straight toward his distant crag. The girl rose to her feet, and, leaning on her paddle, for a moment gazed long and tenderly at the sleeper's face, then softly breathed, "John Norton!"

The call, low as it was, broke through the leaden gates of slumber with the suddenness and effect of a great surprise. Quick as a flash he came to his feet, and, for a moment, stood dazed, bewildered, his bodily powers breaking out of sleep quicker than his senses, and he saw the girl as visitant in vision. He stepped to the water's edge and bathed his face, and turning, freshened and fully awake, saw with glad and apprehensive eyes, who stood before him, and tenderly said:

"Is the daughter of the old race well?"

"Well, well, I am, John Norton," answered the girl, and her voice was low and softly musical, as water falling into water. "I am well, friend of my mother and my friend. And the chief still lives and will live till you come, for so he bade me tell you." And she reached her small hand out to him. He took it in his own, and held it as one holds the hand of child, and answered:

"I am glad. Thou comest like a bird in the night, silently. Why did you not awake me when you came?"

"Why should I wake thee, John Norton?" returned the girl. "I am a day ahead of that the chief set for your coming. For our runner—the swiftest in the woods from Mistassinni to Labrador—said: 'Twelve suns must rise and set before my words could reach thee,' and the chief declared: 'No living man, not even you, could fetch the trail short of ten days.' He timed me to this rock himself, and told me when I would come nor wait another hour, that I would wait by the white rock two days before I saw your face. But I would come, for a voice within me said — a voice which runs vocal in our blood, and has so run through all my race since the beginning of the world — this voice within kept saying: '*Go, for thou shalt find him there!*' And so I, hurrying, came. But tell me how many days were you upon the trail?"

"I fetched the trail in seven days from sun to sun," answered the Trapper, modestly.

"Seven days!" exclaimed the girl, while

the light of a great surprise and admiration shone in her eyes. "Seven days! Thou hast the deer's foot and the cougar's strength, John Norton. No wonder that the war chiefs love you."

And then after a moment's pause:

"But why didst thou push the trail so fiercely?"

"I read your summons and I came," replied the Trapper, sententiously.

The girl started at the hearing of the words, which told her so simply of her power over the man in front of her. Her nostrils dilated, and through the glorious swarth of her cheek there came a flush of deeper red. The gloom of her eyes moistened like glass to the breath. Her ripe lips parted as to the passing of a gasp, and the full form lifted as if the spirit of passion within would fling the beautiful frame it filled upon the strong man's bosom. Thus a moment the sweet whirlwind seized and shook her, then passed. Her eyes drooped modestly, and with a sweet humbleness, as one who has received from heaven beyond her hope or merit, she simply said:

"I have brought you food, John Norton. Come and eat."

The food was of the woods. Bread coarse and brown, but sweet with the full cereal sweetness; corn, parched in the fire, which eaten, lingered long as a rich flavor in the mouth; venison, roasted for a hunter's hunger, within whose crisp surface the life of the deer still showed redly; water from the lake, drunk from a cup shaped from the inner bark of the golden birch, whose hollow curvature still burned with warm chrome colors. So, on the cool lake shore, in the red light of early morn, they broke their fast.

The Trapper ate as a strong man eats after long toil and scant feeding, not grossly, but with a heartiness good to see. The girl ate little, and that absently, as if the atoms in her mouth were foreign to her senses and no taste followed eating.

"You do not eat," said the Trapper. "The sun will darken on the lower hills before we come to food again. Are you not hungry?"

"Last night I was ahungered," answered the girl, musingly. "But now I hunger no more," and her face was as the face of a Madonna holding her child, full of a plentiful and sweet content.

"I do not understand you," returned the Trapper, after a moment's silence. "Your words be plain, but their sense is hidden. Why are you not hungry?"

"You read me once out of your sacred books, John Norton, that man does not live by bread alone, but by every word that proceedeth out of the mouth," responded the girl. "I knew not then the meaning of the words, for I was a girl, and had no understanding, and the words were old, older than your books, and therefore deeply wise, and I, being young, did not know. But I know now." And here the girl paused a moment, hesitated as a young bird to leave the sure bough for the first time, then, rallying courage for the deed, gazed with her large eyes lovingly into his, and timidly explained: —

"I am not hungry John Norton, for God has fed me!"

To the tanned cheek of the Trapper there rushed a glow like the flush to a face of a girl. The light of a happy astonishment leaped from his eyes, and his breath came strongly. Then light and color faded, and as one vexed and heartily ashamed of his vanity, while the lines of his face tightened, he made harsh answer:

"Talk no more in riddles, lest I be a fool, and read the riddle awry. Nor jest again on matters grave as life, lest I, who am but mortal man and slow withal, forget wisdom and take thy girlish playfulness for earnest talk. Nay, nay," he added earnestly, as she rose to her feet with an exclamation of passionate pain, "Say not another word, you have done no ill. You be young and fanciful, and I — I be a fool! Come, let us go. The pull is long, and we shall need the full day's light to reach the island ere night falls." And, placing his rifle in the canoe, he signaled to the hound and seated himself at the oars. The girl obeyed his word, stepped to her place and pushed the light boat from the sands on which so much had been received and so much missed. Perhaps her woman's heart foretold that love like hers would get, even as it gave, all at last.

. . . . .

The house was large and lofty, builded of logs squared smoothly and mortared neatly between the edges. In the thick walls were deep embrasures, that light through the great windows might be more abundant. The builders loved the sun and made wide pathways for its entrance everywhere. The casements, fashioned to receive storm shutters, were proof against winter's wind and lead alike. In the steep roof were dormer windows, glassed with panes, tightly soldered to the sash. At either end of the great house a huge chimney rose, whose solid masonry of stone stood boldly out from the hewn logs, framed closely against its mortared sides. A wide veranda ran the entire length of the southern side. A balustrade of cedar logs, each hewn until it showed its red and fragrant heart, ran completely round it. Above posts of the same sweetly odored wood — whose fragrance, with its substance, lasts forever — was lattice-work of poles stripped of their birchen bark, and snowy white, on which a huge vine ran its brown tracery, enriched with bunches, heavily pendent, of blue-black grapes — that pungent growth of northern woods, whose odors make the winding rivers sweet as heaven. In front, a natural lawn sloped to the yellow sands, on which the waves fell with soft sound.

Eastward, a widely acred field showed careful husbandry. Garnet and yellow colored pods hung gracefully from the brown poles. The ripened corn showed golden through the parted husks, and beds of red and yellow beets patched the dark soil with their high colors. The solar flower turned its broad disk toward the wheeling sun, while dahlias, marigold, and hardy annuals, with their bright colors, warmed like a floral campfire the stretch of gray stubble and pale barren beyond. It was a lovely and a lonely spot, graced by a lordly home, such as the wealthy worthies builded here and there in the great wilderness for comfort and for safety in the old savage days when feudal lords[1] made good their claim to forest seigniories with sword and musket, and every house was home and castle.

The canoe ran lightly shoreward. The beach received its pressure as a mother's bosom receives the child running from afar to its reception — yieldingly; and on the

[1] If the reader will recall that old Canada, viz., the Province of Quebec, was wholly French in origin, and that its organization rested on the feudal basis, the whole territory occupied being divided not into towns and counties, but into seigniories.

welcoming sand the light bark rested. The Trapper stepped ashore and reached his hand back to the girl. Her velvet palm touched his, rough and strong, as thistle-down, wind blown, the oak tree's bark, then nestled and stayed. Thus the two stood hand in hand, gazing up the sloping lawn at the great house, the broad, bright field and the circling forest, glowing with autumnal colors, which made the glorious background. The green lawn, the great gray house, and the vast woods belting it around, brightly beautiful, made such a landscape picture as Titian would have reveled in. It stood, this mansion of the woods, this wilderness castle, in glorious loneliness, a part and centre of a splendid solitude, beyond the coming and going of men, beyond their wars and peace, the creation and embodiment of a mystery deep as the woods around it; a strange, astounding spectacle to one who did not know the history of the forest.

"It is a noble place," exclaimed the Trapper, as he gazed up the wide lawn at the great house, and swept with admiring glance the glorious circle of the woods which curved their belt of splendor round it; "it is a noble place, and if mortal man might find content on earth, he might find it here."

"Could you, John Norton, living here, be content?" inquired the girl, and she lifted the splendor of her eyes to his strong, honest face.

"Content," returned the Trapper, innocently, "why, what more could mortal crave than is here to his hand? A field to give him bread, a noble house to live in, the waters full of fish, the woods of game, the sugar of the maple for his sweetening, honey for his feasts, and not a trap within two hundred miles. What more could mortal man, of good judgment, crave?"

"Is there nothing else, John Norton?" asked the girl.

"Aye, aye," returned the Trapper, "one thing. I did forget the dog. A hunter should have his hound."

A shade of pain, perhaps vexation, came to her face as she heard the Trapper's answer. She withdrew her hand from his and said: "Food, fur, and a house are not enough, John Norton. A dog is good for camp and trail. Solitude is sweet and the absence of wicked men a boon. But these do not make home nor heaven, both of which we crave and both of which are possible on earth, for the conditions are possible. The chief has found this spot a dreary place since mother died."

"Your mother was an angel," answered the Trapper, "and your words are those of wisdom. I have thought at times of the things you hint at, and, as a boy, I had vain dreams, for nature is nature. But I have my ideas of woman and I love perfect things. And I—I am but a hunter, an unlearned man, without education, or house, or land, or gold, and I am not fit for any woman that is fit for me!"

The change that came to the girl's face at the Trapper's words—for he had spoken gravely, and through the honesty of his speech she looked and saw the greatness and humility of his nature — was one to be to him who saw it a memory forever. The shadow left it and its dusky splendor was lighted with the glow of a blessed assurance. This man would love her! This man with the eagle's eye, the deer's foot, the cougar's strength, the honest heart, would love her! This man her mother reverenced, her uncle loved, who twice had saved her life at the risk of his, whose skill and courage were the talk of a thousand camps, whose simple word in pledge held faster than other's oaths — this man into whose very bosom her soul had looked as into a clean place — this man would love her! If heaven be what good men say, and all its bliss had been pledged to her when she lay dying, her body would not have thrilled with a warmer glow than rushed its sweet heat through her veins at that instant of blessed conviction. Wait! She could wait for years, but she would win him—win him to herself; win him from his blindness, which did him honor, to that dazzling light in whose glory man stands but once; but, standing so, sees, with a glad bewilderment, that the woman he dares not love, because she is so infinitely better than he, loves him! Yes, she would win him—win him with such sweet art, such patient approaches, such seductiveness of innocent passion, slowly and deliciously disclosed, that he should never know of his temerity until, thus drawn to her, she held him in her arms irrevocably, in bonds that only cold and hateful death could part. Through all her leaping blood this blessed hope, this sure, sweet knowledge flowed like spiced wine. This man, this man she worshipped, he would love her! It was enough. Her cup ran full to the brim and overflowed. She simply took the Trapper's hand again and said:

"We will go to the chamber of the chief. His eyes will brighten when he sees thy face."

CHAPTER II.

THE FIGHT AT MAMELONS.[1]

"IT was a dreadful fight, John Norton. We went into it a thousand warriors on a side, and in either army were twenty chiefs of fame. We fought the fight at Mamelons, where, at sunset, we met the Esquimaux,[2] coming up as we were going down. The Montaignais headed the war. The Moun-

[1] This old battle-ground is located on the high terraces which define the several sand mounds now standing back of Tadousac.

[2] The Esquimaux were numerous and very warlike, and at one time had pushed their conquests clean up to the Saguenay.

taineers,[1] whose fathers' wigwams stood at Mamelons, had fought the Esquimaux a thousand years, and both had wrongs to right. My father died that summer, and I, fresh from the fields of France, headed my tribe. You know how small it was, the last remnant of the old Lenape root, but every man a warrior. I knew not the right or wrong of it, nor did I care. I only knew our tribe was pledged to the Nasquapees[2] of frozen

[1] The Montaignais Indians held the country, from Quebec down to the Esquimaux, near Seven Islands, and called themselves "Mountaineers."

[2] The Nasquapees are one of the most remarkable families of Indians on the continent, and of whom but little is known. Their country extends from Lake Mistassinni eastward to Labrador, and from Ungava Bay to the coast mountains of the St. Lawrence. They are small in size, fine featured, with mild, dark eyes, and

Ungava, and they were allies of the Mountaineers, and hence the fight held us to its edge. That night we slept under truce, but when the sun came up went at it. I see that morning now. The sun from out the eastern sea rose red as blood. The Nasquapees, who lived as atheists without a Medicine man, cared not for this, but the prophet of the Mountaineers painted his face and body

extremely small hands and feet. The name Nasquapees — Nasqupics — means "a people who stand straight." They have no Medicine man or Prophet, and hence are called by other tribes atheists. Their sense of smell is so acute that it rivals the dog's. "Spirit rappings," and other strange manifestations peculiar to us moderns, have been practised immemorially among them, and carried to such a shade of success that one of our Boston séances would be a laughable and bungling affair to them. Their language is like the Western Crees, and their traditions point to a remote eastern origin.

black as night, tore his blanket into shreds, and lay in the sand as one dead. The Nasquapees laughed, but we of the mountains knew by that dread sign that our faces looked toward our last battle. We made it a brave doom. We fought till noon upon the shifting sands, nor gained an inch, nor did our foes, when suddenly the sun was clouded and a great wind arose that drove the sand so thickly that it hid the battle. The firing and the shouting ceased along the terrace where we fought, and a great, dread silence fell on the mighty mounds, save when the fierce gusts smote them. Thus, living and dead, friend and foe, we lay together, our faces plunged into the coarse gravel, our hands clutching the rounded stones, that we might breathe and stay until the wind might pass.

And such a wind was never blown on man before, for it was hot and came straight down from heaven, so that our backs winced as we lay flattened. Thus, mixed and mingled, we clung to the hot stones, while some crept in beneath the dead for shelter. So both wars clung to the ground for an hour's space. Then, suddenly the sun rushed out, and shaking sand from eyes and hair, and spitting it from our mouths, at it we went again. It was an awful fight, John Norton, and more than once, in the mad midst of it, smoke-blinded and sand-choked, I thought of you and that I heard your rifle crack."

"I would to God I had been there!" exclaimed the Trapper, and he dashed his huge hand into the air, as if cheering a line of battle on, while his eyes blazed and his face whitened.

"I would to God you had been!" returned the chief. "For whether one lived through it, or died in it, we made it great by great fighting. For we fought it to the end in spite of interruptions."

"Interruptions!" exclaimed the Trapper. "I do not understand ye, chief. What but death could interrupt a fight like that?"

"Listen, Trapper, listen," rejoined the chief, excitedly. "Listen, that you may understand what stopped the fight, for never since man was born was fought such fight as we there fought, high up above the sea, that day at Mamelons. I told you it was an old feud between the Mountaineers and Esquimaux, a feud that had held its heat hot for a thousand years, and we, a thousand on each side, one for each year, fought on the sand, while above, below, and around the dead of a thousand years, slain in the feud, fought too."

"Nay, nay," exclaimed the Trapper. "Chief, it cannot be. The dead fight not, but live in peace forever, praise be to God," and he bowed his head reverently.

"That is your faith, not mine, John Norton, for I hold to an older faith — that men by a knife's thrust are not changed, but go, with all their passions with them, to the Spirit-Land, and there build upward on the old foundation. And so, I say again, that the dead of a thousand years fought in the air above and around us on that day at Mamelons. For in the pauses of the wind, we who fought on either side heard shrieks, and shouts, and tramplings as of ten thousand feet, and over us were roarings, and bellowings, and hollow noises, dreadful to hear, and through all the battle went the word that '*the old dead were fighting, too!*' and that made us wild. Both sides went mad. The dying cheered the living, and the living cheered the dead. So went the battle — the fathers and the sons, the dead and living, hard at it. The waters of the Saguenay, a thousand feet below, were beaten into foam by the rush of fighting feet, and the roaring of a great battle filled its mouth. Its dark tide whitened with strange death froth from shore to shore, while ever and anon its surface shivered and shook. And under us on the high crest, cloud-wrapped, the earth trembled as we fought, so that more than once as we stood clinched, we two, the foe and I, still gripped for death, would pause until the ground grew steady, for its tremblings made us dizzy, then clinch the fiercer, mad with a great madness at being stopped in such death-grapple. Under us all the long afternoon the great mounds rose and sank like waves that have no base to stand upon. The clouds snowed ashes. Mud fell in showers. The air we breathed stank with brimstone and burnt bones. And still it thickened, and still both sides, now but a scattered few, fought on, until at last, with a crash, as if the world had split apart, darkness, deep as death, fell suddenly, so that eyes were vain, and we who were not dead, unable to find foe, stood still. And thus the battle ended, even drawn, because God stopped the fight at Mamelons.[1]

. . . . .

[1] The Saguenay is undoubtedly of earthquake origin. The north shore of the St. Lawrence from Cape Tour-

"At last the morning dawned at Mamelons, and never since those ancient beaches[1] saw

mente to Point du Monts, is one of the earthquake centres of the world. In 1663 a frightful series of convulsions occurred, lasting for more than four months; and, it is said, that not a year passes that motions are not felt in the earth. The old maelstrom at Bai St. Paul was caused by subterranean force, and by subsequent shocks deprived of its terrible power. The mouth of the Saguenay was one of the great rendezvous of the Indian races long before Jacques Cartier came, and the great mounds above Tadousac have been the scene of many great Indian battles; but I would not make affidavit that an earthquake ever did actually take place while one was being fought, although there may have been, and certainly, from an artistic point of view, there should have been, such a poetic conjunction.

[1] These mamelons, or great sand mounds, are believed to be the old geologic beaches of earliest times. They rise in tiers, or great terraces, one above the other, to a great height, the uppermost one being a thousand feet or more above the Saguenay, and represent, as they

the world's first morning, had the round sun looked down on such a scene. The great terraces on which we fought were ankle deep with ashes mixed with mud, and cinders black and hard, like burnt iron, and all the sand was soaked with blood. The dead were heaped. They lay like drifted wreckage on a beach, where the eddying surges of the battle tossed them in piles and tangled heaps like jammed timber. For in the darkness, we had fought by sound, and not by sight, and where the battle roared loudest, thither had we rushed, using axe and knife and the short seal spears of the damned Esquimaux. And all the later battle was fought breast to

run down from terrace to terrace, the shrinking of the "face of the deep" in the creative period, by the shrinking of which the solid earth rose in sight.

breast, for ere half were dead, powder and lead gave out, and the fray was hand to hand, until, by the sickening darkness, God stopped it.

"I searched the dreadful field from end to end to find my own, and found them. With blackened hands, clouted with blood, I drew them together. Forty in all, I stretched them, side by side, and the savage pride of the old blood in me burst from my mouth in a shrill yell, when I saw that twenty swarthy bosoms showed the knife's thrust deep and wide. They died like warriors, Trapper, true to the old Lenape blood, whose Tortoise[1] steadfastness upheld the

[1] The Lenni-Lenape had, at the coming of the whites, their territory on the Delaware, but their traditions point to long journeyings from the east over wide waters and cold countries. Their language, strange to

world. I made a mound above their bodies, and heaped it high with rounded stones which crowned the uppermost beach, and made wail above friends and kindred fallen in strange feud. And there they sleep, on that high verge, where the unwritten knowledge of my fathers, told from age to age, declare the waters of the earliest morning first found shore." [See note 1, page 54.]

say, has in it words identical with the old Basque tongue, and establishes some community of origin or history in the remote ages. The Lenni-Lenape had as their Totem, or sacred sign of origin and blood, a Tortoise with a globe on its back, and boasted that they were the oldest of all races of men, tracing their descent through the ages to that day when the world was upheld by a Tortoise, or turtle, resting in the midst of the waters. As a tribe they were very brave, proud, and honorable.

"Never did I hear a tale like this," exclaimed the Trapper. "Strange stories of this fight I heard in the far north, chanted in darkness at midnight, with wild wailing of the tribes; but I held it as the trick of sorcerers to frighten with. Go on and tell me all. Chief, what next befell thee?"

"John Norton, thou hast come half a thousand miles to hear a tale of death told by a dying man. Listen, and remember all I say, for at the close it touches close on thee. A fate whose meshes woven when our blood was crossed has tangled all that bore our name in ruin from the start, and with my going only one remains to suffer further."

Here the chief paused while one might count a score, then, looking steadily at the Trapper, said:

"Last month, when the raven was on the moon,[1] my warning came. The old wound opened without cause, and, lying on this bed, I saw the hour of my death, and beyond, thee, I saw, and beside thee the last and sweetest of our line, and the same doom was over her as has been to us all since the fatal cross — the doom which sends courage and beauty to a quick, sad death."

"I do not understand," replied the Trapper. "Tell me what befell thee further, step by step, and how I, a man without a cross,[2] can be connected with the old traditions of thy tribe and house?"

[1] When the raven was on the moon. An Indian description of an eclipse.

[2] A man without a cross, viz., a pure-blooded man. A white man without any Indian or foreign blood in his veins.

"Listen. In coming from the field, I saw, half-covered by the ashes, a body clothed in a foreign garb. It lay face downward where the dead were thickest, one arm outstretched, the hand of which, gloved to the wrist, still gripped a sword, red to its jeweled hilt. The head was foul with ash and sand, but I noted that the hair was black and long, and worn like a warrior's of our ancient race. Then I remembered a habit of boyish days and pride. Trembling, I stooped, lifted the body upward and turned the dead face toward me. And there, there on that field of Mamelons, where it was said of old, before one of my blood had ever seen the salted shore, the last of our race should die, all foul with ash and sand and blood, brows knit with battle rage, teeth bared and tightly set, *I saw my brother's face!*"

"God in heaven!" exclaimed the Trapper. "How came he there, and who killed him?"

"John Norton, you know our cross, and that the best blood of the old world and the new, older than the old, is in our veins. My grandsire was the son of one who stood next to the throne of France, and all our line have studied in her polished schools since red and white blood mingled in our veins. There did we two, my brother and I, remain until my father called us home. I left him high in the court's favor. Thence, suddenly, without sending word, with a young wife and office of trust, he voyaged, hoping to give me glad surprise. A tempest drove his ship on Labrador; but he saved wife and gold. The

Esquimaux proved friendly, and gave him help, and, reckless of consequence, as have been all our line since the French taint came to us, not knowing cause, he joined the wild horde, and came with them to fatal Mamelons and its dread fight.

"So chanced it, Trapper. I dropped the body from my arms, for a great sickness seized me and my head swam, and in the bloody tangle of dead bodies I sat limp and lifeless. Then in a frenzy, clutching madly at a straw of hope, I tore the waistcoat, corded with gold, from the stiff breast to find proof that would not lie. And there, there above his heart, with eyes bloodshot and bulging, I saw the emblem of our tribe—the Tortoise, with the round world on his back; and through the sacred Totem of our ancient lineage, which our father's hand had tattooed on his chest and mine; yea, through it and the white skin above his heart, there gaped a gash, swollen and red, which my own knife had made. For in the darkness of the fight, bearing up against an Esquimaux rush, ash-blinded, I found a foe who swore in French and had a sword. He and I fought grappling in the dark, when the earth hove beneath our feet and ashes rained upon us; and his sword ran me through even as I thrust my long knife into him.

"And thus at Mamelons, where sits the doom of our race awaiting us, in its dread fight, both fighting without cause, I slew my brother, and from his hand I got the wound from whose old poison I now die.

"Thus I stood among the dead at Mamelons, a chief without a tribe and my brother's murderer. I moved some bodies and scraped downward, that I might have clean sand to fall upon; then drew my knife to let life out, and thus meet bravely the old doom foretold for me and mine as awaiting us since man was born on the shore of that first world. But even as I bent to the knife's point, a voice called me and I turned.

"It was an Esquimau; the only chief left from the fight; my brother's host seeking my brother. He knew me, for he and I had clinched in the great fight, but the earth opening parted us, and so both lived. Each felt for each as warriors feel for a brave foe when the red fight is ended and the field of death is heavy. Thus, battle-tired, amid the dead, we lifted hands, palm outward, and met in peace. He knew the language of old France, and I told him of my woe, of our old race, of tribesmen dead, of brother slain by my own hand, and of the doom that waited for us over Mamelons. And then he spoke and told me that which stayed my hand and held me unto further life.

"Seven days I journeyed with him, and on the eighth I came to where she sat, amid his children, in his rude house at Labrador. Never, since God created woman, was one made so beautiful as she. She was of that old Iberian race, whose birth is older than annals, whose men conquered the world and whose women wedded gods. She was a Basque,[1] and her ancestor's ships had an-

[1] As far back in time as annals or traditions extend, a race of men called Iberians dwelt on the Spanish penin-

chored under Mamelons a thousand years before the Breton came. Fresh from the

sula. Winchell says that "these Iberians spread over Spain, Gaul, and the British islands as early as 5000 B.C. When Egypt was only at her fourth dynasty this race had conquered all the world west of the Mediterranean."

They originally settled Sardinia, Italy, and Sicily, and spread northward as far as Norway and Sweden. Strabo says, speaking of a branch of this race: "They employ the art of writing, and have written books containing memorials of ancient times, and also poems and laws set in verse, for which they claim an antiquity of 6000 years. These old Iberians to-day are represented by the Basques. The Basques are fast dying out, and but a small remnant is left. They undoubtedly represent the first race of men. They are proud, merry, and passionate. The women are very beautiful, and noted for their wit, vivacity, and subtle grace of person. They love music, and dance much. Some of their dances are symbolic and connected with their ancient mysteries. Their language is unconnected with any European tongue dreadful field, with heart of lead, my brother's face staring whitely at me as I talked, I told her all — the fight, the death of brother and of tribe, and the doom that waited for our blood above the shining sands at Mamelons.

or dialect, but, strange to say, it is connected by close resemblance, in many words, with the Maiya language of Central America and that of the Algonquin-Lenape and a few other of our Indian tribes. Duponceau says of the Basque tongue:

"This language, preserved in a corner of Europe by a few thousand Mountaineers, is the sole remaining fragment of perhaps a hundred dialects, constructed on the same plan, which probably existed and were universally spoken at a remote period in that quarter of the world. Like the bones of the mammoth, it remains a monument of the destruction produced by a succession of ages. It stands single and alone of its kind, surrounded by idioms that have no affinity with it."

"She listened to the end. Then rose and took my hand and kissed it, saying: 'Brother, I kiss thy hand as head of our house. What's done is done. The dead cannot come back.' Then, covering up her face with her rich laces, she went within the hanging skins, and for seven days was hidden with her woe.

"But when the seven days were passed she came, and we held council. Next morn, with ten canoes deep laden with gold and precious stuffs, that portion of her dower saved from the wreck, we started hitherward. This island, after many days of voyaging, we reached, and landed here, by chance or fate I know not, for she spake the word that stopped us on this shore, not I. For on this island did my fathers live, and here the fateful cross came to our blood, that cross with

France which was not fit; for the traditions of our tribe—a mystery for a thousand years—had said that any cross of red with white should ripen doom at Mamelons; for there it was the white first landed on the shore of this western world.[1]

[1] The antiquity of European visitation to the St. Lawrence is unascertained, and, perhaps, unascertainable. But there is good reason to think that long before Jacques Cartier, Cabot, or even the Norsemen, ever saw the American continent, the old Basque people carried on a regular commerce in fish and fur with the St. Lawrence. It is not impossible but that Columbus obtained sure knowledge of a western hemisphere from the old race, who dwelt, and had dwelt, immemorially among the mountains of Spain, as well as from the Norse charts. Their language, legends, traditions, and many signs compel one to the conclusion that the old Iberian race, who once held all modern Europe and the British isle in subjection, was of ocean origin, and pushed on the van of an old-time and world-wide navi-

"She needed refuge, for within her life another life was growing. Brooding, she prayed that the new soul within her might not be a boy. 'A boy,' she said, 'must meet the doom foretold. A girl, perchance, might not be held.' Her faith and mine were one, save hers was older, she being of the old trunk stock, of which the world-supporting Tortoise were a branch; and so my blood was later, flowing from noonday fountains, while hers ran warm and red, a pure, sole stream, which burst from out the ponderous front of dead eternity, when, with His living rod, God smote it, in the red sunrise of the

gation beyond the record of modern annals. Both Jacques Cartier and John Cabot found, with astonishment, old Basque names everywhere, as they sailed up the coast, the date of whose connection with the geography of the shores the natives could not tell.

world. On this her soul was set, nor could I change her thought with reason, which I vainly tried, lest if the birth should prove a boy, the shock should kill her. But she held stoutly to it, saying:

"'The women of our race get what they crave. My child shall be a woman, and being so, win what she plays for.'

"And, lo! she had her wish; for when the babe was born it was a girl.

"All since is known to you, for you, by a strange fate, blown, like a cone of the high pine from the midst of whirlwinds, when forest fires are kindled and the gales made by their heat blow hot a thousand miles across the land, dropped on this island like help from Heaven. Twice was I saved from death by thee. Twice was she rescued at the peril of thy life; mother and child, by thy quick hand, snatched out of death. And when the cursed fever came, and she and I lay, like two burning brands, you nursed us both, and from your arms at last, her eyes upon you lovingly, her soul unwillingly, under fate, went from us. And her sweet form, instinct with the old grace and passion of that vanished race which once outrivaled Heaven's beauty and won wedlock with the gods, lay on your bosom as some rare rose, touched by untimely frost, while yet its royal bloom is opening to the sun, lies, leaf loosened, a lovely ruin rudely made on the harsh gravel walk."

Here the chief stopped with a gasp, struck through and through with sharp pains. His face whitened and he groaned. The spasm passed, but left him weak. Rallying, with effort, he went on:

"I must be brief. That spasm was the second. The third will end me. God! How the old stab jumps to-night!

"Trapper, you know how wide our titles reach. A hundred miles from east to west, from north to south, the manor runs. It is a princely stretch. A time will come when cities will be on it, and its deeds of warranty be worth a kingdom. Would that a boy outside the deadly limits of the cross, but dashed with the old blood in vein and skin, were born to heir the place and live as master on these lakes and hills, on which the mighty chiefs who bore the Tortoise sign upon their breasts when it upheld the world, beyond the years of mortal memory, lived and hunted! For when the doom in the far past, before one of our blood had ever seen the salted shore, was spoken, it was said:

"'This doom, for sin against the blood, shall not touch one born in the female line from sire without a cross.'

"I tell you, Trapper, a thousand chiefs of the old race would leave their graves and fight again at Mamelons to see the old doom broken, and a boy, with one clear trace of ancient blood in vein and skin, ruling as master here! And I, who die to-night, I, and he who gave me death and whom I slew, would rise to lead them!

"John Norton, you I have called; you who have saved my life and whose life I have saved; you, who have stood in battle with me when the red line wavered and we two saved the fight; you who have the wild deer's foot, the cougar's strength, whose word once given stands, like a chief's, the test of fire; you, all white in face, all red at heart, a Tortoise, and yet a man without a cross, have I called half a thousand miles to ask with dying breath this question:

"May not that boy be born, the old race kept alive, the long curse stayed, and ended with my life forever be the doom of Mamelons? Speak, Trapper, friend, comrade in war, in hunt and hall, speak to my failing ear, that I may die exultant and tell the thousand chiefs that throng to greet me in the Spirit-land that the old doom is lifted and a race with blood of theirs in vein and skin shall live and rule forever mid their native hills?"

From the first word the strange tale, half chanted, had rolled onward like the great river flooding upward from the gulf, between narrowing banks, with swift and swifter motion, growing pent and tremulous as it flows, until it challenges the base of Cape Tourment with thunder. And not until the dying chief, with headlong haste, had launched the query forth — the solemn query, whose answer would fix the bounds of fate forever — did the Trapper dream whither the wild tale tended. His face whitened like a dead man's, and he stood dumb — dumb with doubt and fear and shame. At last, with effort, as when one lifts a mighty weight, he said, and the words were heaved from out his chest, as great weights from deepest depths: "Chief, ye know not what ye ask. My God! I am not fit!"

Across the swarth face of the dying man there swept a flash of flame, and his glazed eyes lighted with a mighty joy.

"Enough! enough! It is enough!" he cried. "The women of her race will have their way, and she will win thee. God! If I might live to see that brave boy born, the spent fountain of the old race filled again by that rich tide in her which flows red and warm from the sunrise of the world! Nay, nay. Thou shalt not speak again. I leave it in the hands of fate. Before I pass the seeing eye will come, and I shall see if sunlight shines on Mamelons."

He touched a silver bell above his head, and, after pause, the girl, in whom the beauty of her mother and her race lived on, whose form was lithe, but rounded full, whose face was dark as woods, but warmly toned with the old Basque splendor, like wine when light shines through it, type of the two oldest and handsomest races of the world, stood by his side.

Long gazed the chief upon her, a vision too beautiful for earth, too warm for heaven. The light of a great pride was in his eyes, but shaded with mournful pity.

"Last of my race," he murmured. "Last of my blood, farewell! Thou hast thy mother's beauty, and not a trace of the damned cross is on thee. Follow thou thy heart. The women of thy race won so. My 'feet are on the endless trail blazed by my fathers for ten thousand years. I cannot tarry if I would.

I leave thee under care of this just man. Be thou his comfort, as he will be thy shield. There is a chest, thy mother's dying gift, thou knowest where. Open and read, then shalt thou know. Trapper, read thou the ritual of the church above my bier. So shall it please thee. Thou art the only Christian I ever knew who kept his word and did not cheat the red man. Some trace of the old faiths, therefore, there must be in these modern creeds, albeit the holders of them cheat and fight each other. But, daughter of my house, last of my blood, born under shadow, and it may be unto doom, make thou my burial in the old fashion of thy race, older than mine. These modern creeds and mushroom rituals are not for us whose faiths were born when God was on the earth, and His sons married the daughters of men. So bury me, that I may join the old-time folk who lived near neighbors to this modern God, and married their daughters to His sons."

Here paused he for a space, for the old wound jumped, and life flowed with his blood.

Then suddenly a change came to his face. His eyes grew fixed. He placed one hand above the staring orbs, as if to help them see afar. A moment thus. Then, whispering hoarsely, said:

"Take thou his hand. Cling to it. The old Tortoise sight at death is coming. I see the past and future. Daughter, I see thee now, and by thy side, thy arms around his neck, his arms round thee, the man without a cross! Aye. She was right. 'The women of my race get what they crave.' Girl, thou hast won! Rejoice, rejoice and sing. But, oh! my God! My God! John Norton! Look! Daughter, last of my blood, in spite of all, in spite of all, above thy head hangs, breaking black, the doom of Mamelons!"

And with these words of horror on his lips, the chief, whose bosom bore the Tortoise sign, who killed his brother under doom at Mamelons, fell back stone dead.

So died he. Three days went by in silence. Then did the two build high his bier in the great hall, and place him on it, stripped like a warrior, to his waist, for so he charged the Trapper it should be. Thus sitting in the great chair of cedar, hewn to the fragrant heart, in the wide hall, hound at feet, the Tortoise showing plainly on his breast, a fire of great knots, gummed with odorous pitch, blazing on the hearth, the two, each by the faith that guided, made, for the dead chief of a dead tribe, strange funeral.

And first, the Trapper, standing by the bier, gazed long and steadfastly at the dead man's face. Then the girl, going to the mantel, reached for a book and placed it in his hand and stood beside him.

Then, after pause, he read:

"*I am the resurrection and the Life.*"

And the liturgy, voiced deeply and slowly read, as by one who readeth little and labors with the words, sounded through the great hall solemnly.

Then the girl, standing by his side, in the splendor of her beauty, the lights shining warmly on the dark glory of her face, lifted up her voice — a voice fugitive from heaven's.

choir — and sang the words the Trapper had intoned:

"*I am the resurrection and the Life.*"

And her rich tones, pure as note of hermit-thrush cleaving the still air of forest swamps; clear as the song of morning lark singing in the dewy sky, rose to the hewn rafters and swelled against the compressing roof as if they would break out of such imprisonment, and roll their waves of sound afar and upward until they mingled with kindred tones in heaven.

Again the Trapper:

"*He who believeth in me, though he were dead, yet shall he live!*"

And again the marvellous voice pealed forth the words of everlasting hope, as if from the old race that lived in the dawn of the world, whose blood was in her rich and red, had come to her the memory of the music they had heard run thrilling through the happy air when the stars of the morning sang together for joy.

Alas, that such a voice from the old days of soul and song should lie smothered forever beneath the sand of Mamelons!

Thus the first part. For the Trapper, like a Christian man without cross, would give his dead friend holy burial. Then came a pause. And for a space the two sat silent in the great hall, while the pitch knots flamed and flared their splashes of red light through the gloom.

Then rose the girl and took the Trapper's place at the dead man's feet. Her hair, black with a glossy blackness, swept the floor. A jewel, large and lustrous, an heirloom of her mother's race, old as the world, burning with Atlantean flame, a miracle of stone-imprisoned fire, blazed on her brow. The large gloom of her eyes was turned upon the dead man's face, and the sadness of ten thousand years of life and loss was darkly orbed within their long and heavy lashes. Her small, swarth hands hung lifeless at her side, and the bowed contour of her face drooped heavy with grief. Thus she, clothed in black cloth from head to foot, as if that old past, whose child she was, stood shrouded in her form, ready to make wail for the glory of men and the beauty of women it had seen buried forever in the silent tomb.

Thus stood she for a time, as if she held communion with the grave and death. Then opened she her mouth, and in the mode when song was language, she poured her feelings forth in that old tongue, which, like some fragrant fragment of sweet wood, borne northward by great ocean currents out of southern seas, for many days storm tossed, but lodged at last on some far shore and found by those who only sense the sweetness, but know not whence it came, lies lodged to-day upon the mountain slopes of Spain. Thus, in the old Basque tongue, sweet fibre of lost root, unknown to moderns, but soft, and sad, and wild with the joy, the love, the passion of ten thousand years, this child of the old past and the old faiths, lifted up her voice and sang:

"O death! I hate thee! Cold thou art and dreadful to the touch of the warm hand and the sweet lips which, drawn by love's dear habit, stoop to kiss the mouth for the long parting. Cold, cold art thou, and at thy touch the blood of men is chilled and the sweet glow in woman's bosom frozen forever. Thou art great nature's curse. The grape hates thee. Its blood of fire can neither make thee laugh, nor sing, nor dance. The sweet flower, and the fruit which ripens on the bough, nursing its juices from the maternal air, and the bird singing his love-song to his mate amid the blossoms — hate thee! At touch of thine, O slayer! the flower fades, the fruit withers and falls, and the bird drops dumb into the grasses. Thou art the shadow on the sunshine of the world; the skeleton at all feasts; the marplot of great plans; the stench which fouls all odors; the slayer of men and the murderer of women. O death!

I, child of an old race, last leaf from a tree that shadowed the world, warm in my youth, loving life, loving health, loving love. O death! how I hate thee!"

Thus she sang, her full tones swelling fuller as she sang, until her voice sent its clear challenge bravely out to the black shadow on the sunshine of the world and the dread fate she hated.

Then did she a strange thing; a rite known to the morning of the world when all the living lived in the east and the dead went westward.

She took a gourd, filled to the brown brim, and placed it in the dead man's stiffened hand, then laid a rounded loaf beside his knee, and on a plate of copper at his feet—serpent edged, and in the centre a pictured island lying low and long in the blue seas, bold with bluff mountains toward the east, but sinking westward until it ran from sight under the ocean's rim, a marvel of old art in metal working, lost for aye — she placed a living coal, and on it, from a golden acorn at her throat, which opened at touch, she shook a dust, which, falling on the coal, burned rosy red and filled the hall with languorous odors sweet as Heaven. Then, at triumphant pose, she stood and sang:

Water for thy thirst I have given,
  Hurry on! hurry on!
Bread for thy hunger beside thee,
  Speed away! speed away!
Fire for thy need at thy feet,
Mighty chief, fly fast and fly far
To the land where thy father and clans-
    men are waiting.

Odor and oil for the woman thou lovest,
Sweet and smooth may she be on thy breast,
When her soft arms enfold thee.

O death! thou art cheated!
He shall thirst never more;
He shall eat and be filled;
The fire at his feet will revive him;
Oil and odor are his for the woman he loves;
He shall live, he shall live on forever
With his sires and his people.
He shall love and be loved and be happy.

O! death grim and great,
O! death stark and cold,
By a child of the old race that first lived
And first met thee;
The race that lived first, still lives
And will live forever.
By the child of the old blood, by a girl!
Thou art cheated!

CHAPTER III.

THE MOTHER'S MESSAGE.

EVENING was on the woods. The girl, her mother's message in her hands, gift from the chest that owned the golden key, sat reading. And this is what she read:

"My daughter: They tell me I must die. I know it, for a chill, strange to my blood, is creeping through and thickening in my veins. It is the old tale told from the beginning of the world — of warm blood frozen when 'tis warmest, and beauty blasted at its fullest bloom. For I am at that age when woman's nature gives most and gets most from sun and flower, from touch of baby hands and man's strong love, and all the blood within her moves, tremulous with forces whose working makes her pure and sweet, as moves the strong wine in the cask when ripening its red strength and flavor. O daughter of a race that never lied save for a loved one! blood of my blood, remember that your mother died hating to die; died when life was fullest, sweetest, fiercest in her; for life is passionate force, and when full is fierce to crave, to seek, to have and hold, and has been so since man loved woman and by woman was beloved. And so it is with me. A woman, I crave to live, and, craving life, must die.

"Death! how I hate thee! What right hast thou to claim me now when I am at my sweetest? The withered and the wrinkled are for thee. For thee the colorless cheek, the shrivelled breast, the skinny hand that shakes as shakes the leaf, frost smitten to its fall, the lustreless eye, and the lone soul that looketh longingly ahead where wait its loved ones; such are for thee; not I. For I am fair and fresh and full through every vein of those quick forces, which belong to life, and hate the grave. This, that you may know your mother died unwillingly, and dying hated death, as all of the old race and faith have ever done since he first came, a power, a mystery and a curse into the world. For in the ancient annals of our fathers it was written 'that in the beginning of the world there was no death, but life was all in all.' God talked with them as father talks with children; their daughters were married to His sons, and earth and heaven were one.

"Your father was of France, but also of that blood next oldest ours. He was Lenape, a branch blown from that primal tree which was the world's first growth, whose roots ran under ocean before the first world sank; a branch blown far by fate, which, falling, struck deep into the soil of this western world, and, vital with deathless sap, grew and became a tree. This was in ancient days, when thoughts of men were writ in pictures and the round world rested on a Tortoise's back — emblem of water. For the first world was insular, and blue seas washed it from end to end, a mighty stretch, which reached from sunrise into sunset, through many zones. Long after men lost knowledge and the earth was flat, and for a thousand years the Tortoise symbol was an unread riddle save to us of the old blood, who knew the pictured tongue, and laughed to see the later races, mongrel in blood and rude, flatten out the globe of God until it lay flat as their ignorance. Your father was Lenape, who bore upon his breast the Tortoise symbol of old knowledge made safe by sacredness; for the wise men of his race, that the old fact might not be lost, but borne safely on like a dry seed blown over deserts until it comes to water, and, lodging, finds chance to grow into a full flowered, fruitful tree, made it, when they died and knowledge passed, the Totem of his tribe. Thus the dead symbol kept the living fact alive. Nor were there lacking other proofs that his blood was one with mine, though reaching us through world-wide channels. For in his tongue, like flecks of gold in heaps of common sand, were words of the old language, clear and bright with the original lustre, when gold was sacred ornament and had no vulgar use. The mongrel moderns have made it base and fouled it with dirty trade; but in the beginning, and by those of primal blood, who knew they were of heaven, it was a sacred metal, held for God.[1]

[1] Among many of the ancient races gold and silver were sacred metals, not used in commerce, but dedicated as votive offerings, or sent to the temples as dues to the gods. Nothing more astonished and puzzled the natives of Peru and Mexico than the eagerness with which the Spaniards sought for gold, and the high value they put upon it. A West Indian savage traded a handful of gold dust with one of the sailors with

"We met in France, and by French custom were allied. I was a girl, and knew not my own self, and he a boy scarce twenty. Reasons of state there were to prompt our marriage, and so we were joined. He was of our old blood. That drew me, and no other thing, for love moved not within me, but nested calmly in my breast as a young bird, ere yet its wings are grown or it has thrilled with flight, rests in its downy cincture. He died at Mamelons; died under doom. You know the tale. He died and you came, fatherless, into the world.

"You are your mother's child. In face and form, in eye and every look, you are of me

Columbus for some small tool, and then ran as for his life to the woods, lest the sailor should repent his bargain and demand the tool to be given back!

and not of him. The French cross in his blood made weakness, and the stronger blood prevailed. This is the law. A turbid stream sinks with quick ebb; the pure flows level on. The Jews prove this. The ancient wisdom stands in them. The creed, which steals from their old faith, whatever makes it strong, has armed the world against them, but their blood triumphs. The old tide, red and true, unmixed, pure, laughs at these mongrel streams. Strong with pure strength it bides its time. The world will yet be theirs, and so the prophecy of their sacred books be met. Pure blood shall win, albeit muddy veins to-day are boasted of by fools.

"But we are older far than they. The Jews are children, while on our heads the rime of hoary time rests white as snow. Our race was old when Egypt, sailing from our ancestral ports, reached, as a colony, the Nile.[1] From tideless Sea,[2] to the Green Island in the west,[3] from southern Spain to Arctic zones, the old Basque banner waved; while under Mamelons, where waits the doom for insult to pure blood, your fathers anchored ships from the beginning. What loss came to the earth when the gods of the old world, of whom we are, sank under sea and with them took the perfect knowledge! Alas! alas! the chill creeps in and on and I must

[1] It is certain that the Iberian race settled on the Spanish peninsula a long time before the Egyptians, a sister colony from the same unknown parental source, doubtless, began their marvellous structures on the Nile.

[2] The Mediterranean.

[3] Ireland.

hurry! I would make you wise before I die with a wisdom which none save the women of our race might speak or learn.

"You will read this when I am fixed among the women of our race in the great realms where they are queens. For since the first the women of our race have ruled and had their way, whether for good or ill, and both have come to them and through them unto others. And so forever will it be. For beauty is a fate, and unto what 'tis set none know. The issue proves it and naught else. So be it. She who has the glory of the fate should have the courage to bide issue.

"Your body is my body; your face my face; your blood my blood. The warmth of the old fires are in it, and the sweet heat which glows in you will make you understand. You are my child, and being so, I give you of myself. I love. Love as the women of our race and only they may love. Love with a love that maketh all my life so that without it all is death to me. That love I, dying, bestow on you. It came to me like flash of fire on altar when holy oils are kindled and the censer swung. Here I first met him. Death had me. He fought and took me from his hand. In the beginning, men were large and strong, and women beautiful. Giants were on the earth, and our mothers wedded them. Each was a rose, thorn-guarded, and the strongest plucked her when in bloom and wore her, full of sweets, upon his bosom. Since then the women of our blood have loved large men. Weak ones we hated. None save the mighty, brawny, and brave have ever felt our soft arms round them, or our mouths on theirs. Thus has it been.

"I loved him, for his strength was as the ancients, and with it gentleness like the gods. But he was humble, and knew not his own greatness, and, blinded by humility, he would not see that I was his. So I waited, waited as all women wait, that they may win. It is not art, but nature, the nature of a rose, which, daily opening more and more to perfect bloom in his warm light, makes the sun know his power at last. For love reveals all greatness in us, as it does all faults. Well did I know that he should see at last his fitness for me, and, without violence to himself, yield to my loveliness and be drawn within the circle of my arms.

So should I win at last, as have the women of our race won always. But death mars all. So has it been since women lived. His is the only knife whose edge may cut the silken bands we wind round men. Vain is all else. Faiths may not stand against us, nor pride, nor honor. Our power draws stronger. The grave alone makes gap 'twixt lovely woman's loving and bridal bed. So, dying thus before my time I am bereft of all.

"But you shall win, for in you I shall live again and to full time. I know that you will love him, for you drew my passion to you with my milk, and all my thoughts were of him, when, with large receptive eyes, you lay a baby in my arms, day after day, scanning my face, love-lighted for him. Aye, you will love him. For in your sleep, cradled on the heart that worshiped him, its warmth for him warmed you, its beating thrilled, and from my mouth, murmured caressingly in dreams, your ears and tongue learned his dear name before mine own. So art thou fated unto love as I to death. Both could not win, and hence, perhaps, 'tis well I die. For had both lived, then both had loved, mother and child been rivals, and one suffered worse than dying. Nor am I without joy. For once, when I was wooing him with art he did not know, coaxing him up to me with sweet praises sweetly said, and purposely I swayed so my warm body fell into his arms and there lay for a moment, vibrant, all aglow, while all my woman's soul went through my lifted and dimmed eyes to him, I saw a flash of fire flame in his face, and felt a throb jump through his body, as the God woke in him, which told me he was mortal. And, faint with joy, I slid downward from his arms and in the fragrant grasses sat, throbbing, covering up my face with happy hands lest he should see the glory of it and be frightened at what his touch had done. I swear by the old blood, that moment's triumph honored, that the memory of that blissful time takes from death its sting and robs the grave of victory, as I lie dying.

"Yea, thou shalt win. The power will be in thee, as it has been in me, to win him or any whom women made as we set heart on. But woo him with that old art of innocence, snow white, though hot as fire, lost to the weak or brazen women of these mongrel races that fill the world to-day, who dare not dare, or daring, overdo. Be slow as sunrise. Let thy love dawn on him as morning dawns upon the earth, and warmth and light grow evenly, lest the quick flash blind him, or the sudden heat appall, and he see nothing right, but shrink from thee and his new self as from a wicked thing. I may not help thee. What fools these moderns are to think so. The dead have their own lives and loves, and note not the living. Else none might be at peace or know comfort above the sky, and all souls would make wail for wrongs and woes done and borne under sun. So is it well that parting should be parting, and what wall divides the dead from living be beyond penetration. For each woman's life is sole. Her plans are hidden with her love. Her skill is of it a sweet secrecy, and all her winning is self-won. I do not fear. Thou wilt have the wooing wisdom of thy race. Thy eyes are such as men give life to look into. The passion in thy blood would purchase thrones. Thou hast the grace of form which maddens men. Thy voice is music. Thy touch warm velvet to the skin. The first and perfect woman lives complete, in thee!

"No more. In the old land no one is left. The modern cancer eats all there. New fashions and new faiths crowd in. Only low blood is left, and that soon yields to pelf and pain. Last am I of the queenly line and thou art last of me. I came of gods. To gods I go. The tree that bore the fruit of knowledge for our sex in the sunrise of the world is stripped to the last sweet leaf. If thou shalt die leaving no root, the race God made is ended. With thee the gods quit earth, and the old red blood beats back and upward to the skies. Gold hast thou and broad acres. Youth and health are thine. Win his great strength to thee, for he is pure as strong, and from a primal man get perfect children, that in this new world in the west a new race may arise rich in old blood, born among the hills, strong with the strength of trees, whose sons shall be as mountains, and whose daughters as the lakes, whose loveliness is lovelier because of the reflected mountains dimly seen in them.

"Farewell. Love greatly. It is the only way that leadeth woman to her heaven. The moderns have a saying in their creed that God is love. In the beginning he was Father. The race that sprang from Him said that, and said no more. It was enough. Love then was human, and we gloried in it. Not the pale love of barren nun, but love red as the rose, warm as the sun, the love of motherly women, sweet mouthed, deep breasted, voiced with cradle songs and soft melodies which made men love their homes. Love thou and live on the old level. Be not ashamed to be full woman. Love strength. Bear children to it. Be mother of a mighty race born for this western world. Multiply. Inherit; and send the old blood flowing from thy veins, a widening current, thrilling through the ages; that it may be as red, as pure, as strong at sunset as it was in the sunrise of the world.

"Once more, farewell, sweet daughter. These are last words, a voice from out the sunset, sweet and low as altar hymn wandering down the columned aisles of some old temple. So may it sound to thee. So live, so woo, so win, that when thou comest through the portals of the west to that fair throne amid those other ones which stretch their stateliness across the endless plain of ended things, which waits for thee as one has waited for every woman of our queenly line, thou shalt leave behind at going a new and noble race, from thee and him, in which the east and west, the sunrise and the sunset of the world shall, like two equal glories, meet condensed and shine. So fare thee well. Fear not Mamelons. For if thou failest there, thou shalt be free of fault, and all the myriad millions of our blood shall out of sunset march, and from the shining sands of fate lift thee high and place thee on the last, the highest, and the whitest throne of our old line. So ends it. One more sweet kiss, sweet one. One more long look into his face—grave, grave and sad he gazeth at me. God! What a face he has! Shall I find match for it to-morrow when I stand, amid the royal, beyond sunset? Perhaps. Death, you have good breeding. You have waited well. Come, now, I will go on with thee. Yes, yes, I see the way. 'Tis very plain. It has been hollowed by so many feet. Good-bye to earthly light and life. It may be I shall find a better. I'll know to-morrow."

Here the scroll ended. Long the living sat pondering what the dead had writ. She kissed the writing as it were holy text. Then placed it in the chest, and turned the golden key and said: "Sweet mother, thou shalt live in me. Our race shall not die out. My love shall win him." Then went she to the great room wherein the Trapper by the red fire sat and said: "John Norton, thou art my guest. What may I do to pleasure thee? Here thou must stay until my mind can order out my life and make the dubious road ahead look plain. While underneath my roof, I pray, command me."

All this with such grave dignity and sweet grace as she were queen and he some kinsman, great and wise.

The Trapper stooped and lifted a huge log upon the fire, which broke the lower brands. The chimney roared, and the large room brightened to the flame. Then, facing her, he said:

"Guest I am and servant, both in one, and must be so awhile. Winter is on us. The fire feels snow. It putters as if the flakes were falling in it. It is a sign that never lies. Hark! you can hear the konk of geese as they wedge southward. The winter will be long, but I must stay."

"And are you sorry you must stay?" replied the girl. "I will do what I may to make the days and nights pass swiftly."

"Nay, nay, you do mistake," returned the Trapper. "I am not sorry for myself, but thee. If I may only help thee: how can I help thee?"

"John Norton," replied the girl, and she spoke with sweet earnestness as when the heart is vocal, "thou art a man, and wise; I am a girl, and know nought save books.

But you, you have seen many men and tribes of men; counciled with chiefs, been comrade with the great, sharing their inner thoughts in peace and war, and thou hast done great deeds thyself, of which fame speaks widely. Why do you cheapen your own value so, calling thyself a common man? My uncle said you were the best, the bravest, and the wisest man he ever met, and he had sat with kings and chiefs, and heard the best men of both worlds tell all they knew. Dear friend, wilt thou not be my teacher, and teach me that, which lieth now, like treasure hidden, locked in thy silence?"

"I teach thee!" exclaimed the Trapper. "I, an unlettered man, a hunter of the woods, teach one who readeth every tongue, who knoweth all the past, to the beginning of the world, whose head has in it all these shelves of knowledge," and the Trapper swept a gesture toward the thousand books that thickened the great hall from floor to ceiling. "I teach thee!"

"Yes, you," answered the girl. "You can teach me, or any woman that ever lived, or any man. For you were given at your birth the seeing eye, the listening ear, and the still patience of the mountain cat, which on the bare bough sits watching, from sunset until sunrise, motionless. In the old days such gifts meant wisdom, wider, deeper, more exact than that of books, for so my mother often told me. She said the wisest men who ever lived were those who, in deep woods and caves and on the shore of seas, saw, heard, and pondered on the life and mysteries of nature, noting all things, small and great, cause and effect, tracing out connections which interlace the parts into one whole, so making one solid woof of knowledge, covering all the world of fact and substance in the end. And once, when you were in the mood, and had been talking in the hall, drawn on and out by her, you told of climes and places you had seen, and strange things met in wandering, of great mounds builded by some ancient race, long dead; of cities, under sunset, still standing solid, without men; of tall and shapely pillars, writ with mystic characters, on the far shore of the mild sea, whence sailed the old dead of my race, at dying, far away to western heavens, where to-day they live; of caverns in deep earth, made glorious with crystals, stalactites, prisms, and shining ornaments, where, in old time the gods of the under world were chambered; of trees that mingled bloom and fruitage the long year through, and flowers that never faded till the root died out; of creeping reptiles, snakes, and savage poisonous things that struck to kill, and of their antidotes, growing for man and beast amid the very grasses where they secreted venom; of rivers wide and deep, boiling up through solid earth, full-tided, which, flowing widely on, dropped suddenly like a plummet to the centre of the world; of plains, fenced by the sky, far reaching as the level sea, so that the red sun rose and set in grasses; of fires which, lit by lightning, blackened the stars with smoke and burned all the world; of oceans in the west, which, flowing with joint floods, fell over mountains, plunging their weights of water sheer downward, so that the rocky framework of the round earth shook; of winds that blew as out of chaos, revolving on a hollow axis like a wheel buzzing, invisible, charged to the centre with electric force, and fires which burst explosive, kindling the air like tinder; and of ten thousand marvels and curious things, which you have met, noted, and pondered on, seeking to know the primal fact or force which underlaid them. So that my mother said that night, when we were in our chamber, that you were the wisest man she ever met; wise with the wisdom of her ancient folk, whose knowledge lived, oral and terse, before the habit of bookmaking came to rive the solid substance, heavy and rich, into thin veneer, to make vain show for fools to wonder at. Teach me! Who might thou not teach, thou seeing, silent man, type of my first fathers, who, gifted with rare senses and with wit to question nature and to learn mastered all wisdom before books were."

"Aye, aye," returned the Trapper, not displeased to hear her praise as rare what seemed to him so common, "these things I know in truth, for I have wandered far, seen much, and noted closely, and he who sleeps in woods has time to think. But, girl, I am an unlearned man, and know naught of books."

"Books!" exclaimed the girl. "What are books but oral knowledge spread out in words which lack the fire of forceful utterance? But you shall know them. The winter days are short, the nights are long; our toil is simple; wood for the fire, food for the table, and a swift push each day along the snow for exercise; or, if the winds will keep some acres clean, our skates shall ring to the smitten ice, piercing it with tremblings till all the shores cry out. All other hours for sleep and books. I read in seven tongues, one so old that none save I in all the world can read it; for it was writ when letters were a mystery, known only unto those who fed the sacred fire and kept God's altars warm. And I will read you all the wisdom of the world, and its rare laughter, which, mother said, was the fine effervesce of wisdom, the pungent foam and sparkle of it. So you shall know. And one old scroll there is, rolled in foil of gold, sealed with the serpent seal, symbol of eternity, scribed with pictured knowledge, an heirloom of my race, whose key alone I have, writ in rainbow colors, when the world was young, the language of the gods, who first made signs for speech and put the speaking mouth upon a page. It was the first I learned. My mother taught it to me standing at her knee — for so the law says it shall be done, a law old with twice ten thousand years of age — that he who knows this scroll shall teach it, under silence, to his or her first born, standing at knee, that the old knowledge of prime things and days may not perish from the earth it tells of, but live on forever while the earth endures. For on it is the record of the beginning, told by those who saw it; of the first man and how he came to be; of woman, first, when born and of what style. A list of healing simples, antidotes 'gainst death, and of rare oils which search the bones and members of the mortal frame and banish pain; and others yet, sweet to the nose, and volatile, that make the face to shine, for feasts and happy days, and being poured on women, make their skin softer than down, whiter than drifted snow, and so clean and clear that the rich blood pinks through it like a red rose centred in crystal. And on it, too, is written other and strange rules, wild and weird. How one may have the seeing eye come to him. How to call up the wicked dead from under ground, and summon from their heaven in the west, where they live and love, the blessed. How marriage came to man with woman. What part is his to act and what part hers, that each may be a joy to other, and she thus honored, be as sweet slip grafted on a vital trunk, full flowered in fullest growth, and fruitful of what the old gods loved, children, healthy, fair, and strong; all will I read thee, talking as we read, that we, with sharpened thought, may bite through to the vital gist, deep centred within the hard rind of words, and taste the living sweetness of true sense. So will we teach each other and grow wise equally; you, me the knowledge of things and places you have seen; I, you the knowledge writ in books that I have read."

CHAPTER IV.

LOVE'S VICTORY.

NEXT day, the Trapper's sign proved true. Winter fell whitely on the world. Its soft fleece floated downward to the earth whiter than washed wools. The waters of the lake blackened in contrast to the shores. The flying leaves — tardy vagrants from the branch — were smothered 'mid the flakes, and dropped like shot birds. Toward night the wind arose. The forest moaned. At sunset, in the gray gloom, a flock of ducks roared southward through the whirling storm. A field of geese, leaderless, bewildered, blinded by the driving flakes, scented water, and, like a noisy mob, fell, with a mighty splash, into the lake. Summer went with the day, and with the night came winter, white, cold, and stormy, roaring violently through the air.

In the great hall sat the two. The logs on the wide hearth piled high, glowed red — a solid coal from end to end, cracked with concentric rings. They reddened the hall, books, skins, and antlered trophies of the chase. The strong man and the girl's dark face stood forth in the warm luminance, pre-Raphaelite. The Trapper sat in a great chair, built solidly of rounded wood, untouched by tool, but softly cushioned. The girl, recumbent, rested on a pile of skins, black with the glossy blackness of the bear, full furred. Her dress, a garnet velvet, from the looms of France. Her moccasins, snow white. On either wrist a serpent coil of gold. A diamond at her throat. A red fez on her head, while over her rich dress the glossy masses of her hair fell tangled to her feet. She read from an old book, bound with rich plush, whose leaves were vellum, edged with artful garniture and lettered richly with crimson ink — a precious relic of old literature, saved from those vandal flames which burned the stored knowledge of the world to ashes at Alexandria. The characters were Phœnician, and told the story of that race to which we owe our modern alphabet; whose ships, a thousand years before the Christ, went freighted with letters, seeking baser commerce, to every shore of the wide world. She read by the fire's red light, and the ruddy glow fell vividly on the pictured page, the rich dress outlining her full form and the swarth beauty of her face. It was the story of an old race — no library has it now — the story of their rise, their glory, and their fall. She read for hours, pausing here and there to tell her listener of connecting things — of Rome that was not then; of Greece yet to be born; of Egypt, swarming on the Nile and building monuments for eternity, and of her ancient race, west of the tideless sea, whose annals, even then, reached backward through ten thousand years, thus making clear what otherwise were dark, and teaching him all history. So passed the hours till midnight struck. Then she arose, and lifting goblet half-filled with water, poured it on the hearth, saying: "I spill this water to a race whose going emptied half the world." This solemnly, for she was of the past, and held to its old fashions, knowing all its symbolism, its rites, its daily customs, and what they meant, for so she had been taught, and nothing else, by her whose blood and beauty she repeated. Then took the Trapper's hand and laid it on her head, bent low, and said: "Dear friend, I am so glad to serve you. I have enjoyed this night beyond all nights I ever knew. I hope for many others like to it, and even sweeter." And saying this she looked with glad and peaceful eyes into his face, and glided noiselessly from the room.

The Trapper piled high the logs again, and, lying down upon the skins where she had lain, gazed with wide eyes into the coals. The gray was in the sky before he slept, and in his sleep he murmured: "It cannot be. I am an unlearned man and poor. I am not fit." Above him in her chamber, nestling in sleep, the girl sighed in her dreams and murmured; "How blind he is!" And then: "My love shall win him!"

Dear girl, sweet soul of womanhood, gift to these gilded days from the old solid past, I would the thought had never come to me to tell this tale of Mamelons!

So went the winter; and so the two grew upward side by side in knowledge. He learning of the past as taught in books; of men long dead whose names had been unknown to him; of deeds done by the mighty of the world; of cities, monuments, tombs long buried; of races who mastered the world and died mastered by their own weaknesses; of faiths, philosophies, and creeds once bright and strong as fire, now cold and weak as sodden ashes; of vanished rites and mysteries and lost arts which once were the world's wonder—all were unfolded to him, so that his strong mind grasped the main point of each and understood the whole. And she learned much from him; of bird and beast and fish; of climates and their growths; of rocks and trees; of nature's signs and movements by day and night; of wandering tribes and mongrel races; the lore of woods and waters and the differences in governments which shape the lives of men. So taught they each the other; she, swift of thought and full of eastern fire; he, slower minded, but calm, sagacious, comprehensive, remembering all and settling all in wise conclusion. Two better halves, in mind and soul and body, to make a perfect whole, were never brought by fate together since God made male and female. The past and present, fire and wood, fancy and judgment, beauty to win and strength to hold, sound minds in sound bodies, the perfect womanhood and manhood ideal, typical, met, conjoined in them.

Slowly she won him. Slowly she drew him, with the innocence of loving, to oneness in wish and thought and feeling, with her sweet self. Slowly, as the moon lifts the great tide, she lifted him toward her, until his nature stood highest, full flooded, nigh, bathed in all the wide, deep flowing of its greatness, in her white radiance. It was an angel's mission, and all the wild passion of her blood, original, barbaric, was sobered with reverent thought of the great destiny that she, wedded to him, stood heir to. She had no other hope, nor wish, nor dream, than to be his. She was all woman. This life was all to her. She had no future. If she had, she wisely put it by until she came to it. She took no thought of far to-morrow. Sufficient for the day was the joy or sorrow of it. She lived. She loved. That was enough. What more might be to woman than to live, to love, worship her husband and bear children? Such life were heaven. If other heaven there were she could not crave it, being satisfied. So felt she. So had she felt. So acted that it might be; and now, at last, she stood on that white line each perfect woman climbs to, passing which, radiant, content, grateful, she enters — heaven.

. . . . .

Spring came. Heat touched the snow, and it grew liquid. The hills murmured as with many tongues, and low music flowed rippling down their sides. The warm earth sweetened with odors. Sap stirred in root and bough, and the fibred sod thrilled with delicious passages of new life.

From the far South came flaming plumage, breasts of gold and winged music to the groves. The pent roots of herbs, spiced and pungent, burst upward through the moistened mould, and breathed wild, gamy odors through the woods. The skeleton trees thickened with leaf formations, and hid their naked grayness under green and gold. Each day birds of passage, pressed by parental instinct, slanted wings toward the lake, and, sailing inward, to secluded bays, made haste to search for nests. Mother otters swam heavy through the tide, and the great turtles, lumbering from the water, digged deep pits under starlight, in the sand, and cunningly piled their pyramid of eggs. All nature loved and mated, each class of life in its own order, and God began the re-creation of the world.

The two were standing under leafy screen on the lake's shore, the warm sun overhead and the wide water lying level at their feet. Nature's mood was on them, and their hearts, like equal atmospheres, flowed to sweet union. Reverently they spoke, as soul to soul, concealing nothing, having nothing to conceal, of their deep feeling and of duty unto each. The girl held up her clean, sweet nature unto him, that he might see it, wholly his forever; and he kept nothing back. She knew he loved her, and to her the task to make him feel the honor she received in being loved by him. So stood they, alone in the deep woods, apart from men, in grave, sweet counsel. Thus spake the man:

"I love you, Atla; you know it. I would lay down my life for you. But our marriage may not be. I am too old."

"Too old!" replied the girl. "Thou hast seen forty years, I twenty. Thou art the riper, sweeter, better; that is all. I would not wed a boy. The women of our race have wedded men, big bodied, strong to fight, to save, to make home safe, their country free, and fame, that richest heritage to children. My mother broke the rule, and rued it. She might have rued it worse had death not cut the tightening error which knotted her to coming torture. My heart holds hard to the old law made for the women of our race by ancient wisdom; 'Wed not boys, but wed grave and gentle men. For women would be ruled, and who, of pride and fire, would be ruled by striplings?' And again: 'Let ivy seek the full-grown oak, nor cling to saplings.' I love the laws that were, love the old faiths and customs. They filled the world with beauty and brave men. They gave great nature opportunity to keep great, kept noble blood from base, strength from wedding weakness, and barred out mongrelism from the world, which in the ancient days was deadliest sin, corrupting all. O love! you do mistake, saying 'I am too old.' For women have ever the child's habit in them. They love to be held in arms, love to look up to loving eyes, love to be commanded, and obey strong sovereignty. The husband is head—head of the house. He sits in wide authority, and from his wisdom flow counsel, command, which all the house, wife, children, and servants, bend to, obedient. How can a stripling fill such seat? How sit such dignity on a beardless face? How, save from seasoned strength, such safety come to all? O full grown man! be oak to me, and let me twine my weakness round thy strength, that I may find safe lodgment, nor be shaken in my roots when storms blow strong. Too old! I would thy head were sown with the white rime of added years. So should I love thee more!"

Ah me, such pleading from love's mouth,

such sweet entreaty from love's heart man never heard before, in these raw days, when callow youth is fondled by weak women, and boys with starting beards push wisdom, gray and grave, from council chairs.

Then, in reply, the Trapper said:

"Atla, it cannot be. I will admit that you say, sooth, my years do not forbid. Boys are rash, hot-headed, quick of tongue, ill-mannered, lacking patience, just sense, and slow-mannered gentleness which comes with added years, and that deep knowledge which slows blood and gentles speech, and I do see that you fit well to these, and would be happier with a man thus charactered. But, letting that go by — and all my heart is grateful that it may — still marriage may not be between us, for thou art rich and I am poor, and so it should not be. For husband should own house; the wife make home. What say you, am I right or wrong?"

To which the girl made answer: "Thou art an old-time man, John Norton, and this judgment fits the ancient wisdom. For in the beginning so it was. The male built nest, the female feathered it with song. So each had part in common ministry. The man was greater, richer, than the woman, and with earthly substance did endow. And she in turn gave sweet companionship, and sang loneliness from his life with mother songs and children's prattle. Thus in the beginning. Yea, thou art right, as thou art always right. For, being sound in heart and head, thou canst not err. Thy judgment goes straight to the centre of the truth as goes thy bullet. But as men lived and died, change came to the first order. For men without male issue died and left great dower to girls. Women, by no fault of theirs, nor lack of modesty, grew rich by gifts of death, which are the gifts of fate. And changing circumstance changed all, making the old law void. The gods pondered, and a new order rose. By chance, at first, then by ordainment, royalty left male and followed female blood, because their blood was truer to itself, less vagrant, purer, better kept. And women of red blood and pure, clothed in royalty from shame, made alliances with men whom their souls loved, and gave rank, wealth, and their sweet selves in lavishness of loving, which gives all and keeps nothing back. Such was the habit of my race and line from age to age, even as I read you from the pictured scroll, rolled in foil of gold, that only I, of all the world, can read; and if I die, leaving no child, the golden secret goes with me to the gods, and all the ancient lore is lost to men forever. This to assist your judgment and make the scales hang level from your hand for just decision. Am I to blame because I stand as heir to ancient blood and wealth? Shall these wide acres, gold in yonder house, gems in casket, and diamonds worn for ten thousand years by women of my race, queens of the olden time, when in their hands they lifted world-wide sceptres, divide thee and me? Has love no weight in the just scales you, by the working of some old fate, I know not what, hold over me and my soul's wish to-day? Be just to your own soul, be just to mine, and fling these doubts aside as settled forever by the mighty Power that works in darkness, and through darkness, to the light, shaping our fates and ordering life and death, joy and grief, beyond our power to fix or change. Blown by two winds, whose coming and going we list not, we, two, meet here. Strong art thou and I am weak, but shall thy strength repel my weakness? Rich, without fault, I am. My blood is older than these hills, purer than yonder water, and wilt thou make an accident, light as a feather in just balances, outweigh a fact sweet as heaven, heavy as fate? The queens of old, whose blood is one with mine, who spake the self-same tongue and loved the self-same way, chose men to be their kings; so I, by the same law, choose thee. Be thou my king.

Rule me in love. By the old right and rule of all my race, I place thy hand upon my head, and so pass under yoke. I am thy subject, and all my days shall be a sweet subjection. Do with me as thou wilt. I make no terms. My feet shall walk with thine to the dark edge of death. Further I know not. This life we may make sure. The next is or is not ours to order. No man may say. Lord of my earthly life, take me, take me to thy arms, that I, last of an old race, last of its blood, left sole in all the world, without father, mother, friend, may feel I am beloved by him I worship, and drink one glad, sweet cup before I go to touch the bitter edge of dubious chance at Mamelons."

Then love prevailed. Doubt went from out his soul. His nature, unrestrained, leaped up in a red rush of joy to eyes and face. He lifted hands and opened arms to her. To them she swept, as bird into safe thicket, chased by hawk, with a glad cry. Panting she lay upon his bosom, trembling through all her frame, placed mouth to his and lost all sense but feeling. Then, with a gasp, drew back and lifted dewy eyes to his, as fed child to nursing mother's face, or saint her worshiping gaze to God.

But the gods of her old race, standing beyond sunset, lifted high, saw, farther on, the sandy slope of Mamelons, and, while she lay in heaven on her lover's breast, they bent low their heads and wept.

. . . .

Spring multiplied its days and growths. Night followed night as star follows star in their far circuits, wheeling forever on. Each morn brought sweet surprise to each. For like the growths of nature so grew their love fuller with bloom each morn; with fragrance fuller each dewy night. Her nature, under love's warmth, grew richer, seeding at its core for sweeter, larger life. His borrowed tone and color from her own, and fragrance. So, in the happy days of the long spring, as earth grew warmer, sweeter with the days, the two grew, with common growth and closer, until they stood in primal unity, no longer twain, but one.

One day she came, and put her hand in his and said:

"Dear love, there is an old rite by which my people married. It bindeth to the grave; no farther. For there the old faith stopped, not knowing what life might be beyond, or by whom ordered. Thine goeth on through death as light through darkness, and holds the hope that earthly union lasts forever. It may be so. Perhaps the Galilean knew better than the gods what is within the veil, for so the symbol is. It is a winning faith. My heart accepts it as a happy chance; and, did it not, it would not matter. Thy faith is mine, and thine shall be my God. Perchance the ancient deities and your modern One are but the same, with different names. We worshiped ours with fruits and flowers and incense; with dancing feet, glad songs, and altars garlanded with flowers; moistened with wine; you, yours with doleful music, bare rites, the beggary of petition and cold reasoning. Ours was the better fashion, for it kept the happy habits up of children, gladly grateful for father gifts, and so prolonged the joyous childhood of the world. But in this thy faith is better — it hangs a star above the tide of death for love to steer by. My heart accepts the sign. Thy faith is mine. We will go down to Mamelons, and there be married by the holy man who wears upon his breast the sign you trust to."

"Nay, nay; it shall not be," exclaimed the Trapper. "Atla, thou shalt not go to Mamelons. There waits the doom for the mixed blood. There died thy father, and all its sands are full of moldering men. We will be married here by the old custom of thy people, and God, who looketh at the heart and knoweth all, will bless us."

"Dear love," returned the girl, "thy word is law to me. I have no other. It shall be as thou wilt. But listen to my folly or my wisdom, I know not which it is: I fear not Mamelons. There is no coward blood in me. The women of our race face fate with open eyes. So it has been from the beginning. Death sees no pallor in our cheeks. To love we say farewell, then graveward go with steady steps. The women of my house — a lengthy line, stretching downward from the past beyond annals — whose blood flows red in me, lived queens, and, dying, died as they lived. I would die so; lest, if thy faith is true, they would not own me kin nor give me place among them when I came, if I feared fate or death. Besides, the doom may not hold good toward me. I know my uncle saw the sight; but he was only Tortoise, a branch blown far from the old tree and lost a thousand years amid strange peoples, and his sight could not, therefore, be sure. Moreover, love, if the curse holds, and I am under doom, how may I escape? For fate is fate, and he who runs, runs quickest into it. So let us go, I pray, to Mamelons, and there be married by the holy man, the symbol[1] on whose breast was known to our old race and carved on altars ten thousand years before the simple Jew was born

[1] The cross as a symbol is traceable through all the old races, even the remotest in point of time. It was originally a symbol of plenty and joy, and so stood emblematic of happiness for tens of thousands of years. The Romans connected it with their criminal law, as we have the gallows, and so it became a symbol of shame and sorrow.

at Bethlehem. So shall the symbol of the old faith and the new be for the first time kissed by two who represent the sunrise and the sunset of the world; and the god of morning and of evening be proved to be the same, though worshiped under different names."

He yielded, and the two made ready to set face toward Mamelons.

. . . .

There was, serving in her house, an old red servitor, who had been chief, in other days, of Mistassinni.[1] His dwindled tribe

[1] This lake lies to the northwest of Lake St. John some 300 miles, and within some 200 miles of James' Bay. It was first discovered by white men in the person of Père Abanel, in 1661, a Jesuit missionary, en route to Hudson's Bay. This is the lake about which so much has been said in Canada and the States, and so much printed. In fact, very little is accurately known of it,

lives still upon the lake which reaches northward beyond knowledge. But he, longer than her life, had lived in the great house,

unless we assume that the late survey by Mr. Low is to be regarded as a settlement of the matter — which few, if any, acquainted with the Mistassinni question would do. Having examined all the data bearing on the subject, I can but conclude that the bit of water which Mr. Low said he surveyed was only a small arm or branch of the lake reaching south from it, and that the Great Mistassinni itself was never seen by Mr. Low, much less surveyed. Unless we concluded with an ancient cynic that "All men are liars," then there surely is a vast body of water known to the natives as Big Mistassinni, lying in the wilderness several hundreds of miles from Hudson's Bay, yet to be visited and surveyed by white men. Mista, in Indian dialect, means great, and sinni means a stone or rock. And hence Mistassinni means the "Lake of Great Stones or Rocks." The Assinniboine, or Rocky River, Indians of the West were evidently of the same blood and language originally with these red men of the northern wilds.

a life-long guest, but serving it in his wild fashion. Warring with Nasquapees and Mountaineers against the Esquimaux, he had been overcome in ambush and in the centre of their camp put to the torture. Grimly he stood the test of fire, not making moan as their knives seamed him and the heated spear points seared. Maddened, one pried his jaws apart with edge of hatchet, and tore his tongue out, saying, in devilish jest, "If thou wilt not talk, thou hast no need of this," and ate it before his eyes. Then the Chief, with twice a hundred braves, burst in upon them, and whirled the hellish brood, in roaring battle, out of the world. The Trapper, plunging through whirring hatchets and red spear points, sent the cursed fagots flying that blazed upward to his bloody mouth and so saved him to the world. Crippled beyond hope of leadership, he left his tribe, and, toiling slowly through the woods, came to the Chief in the great house and said, in the quick language of silent signs: "I am no longer chief — I cannot fight. Let me stay here until I die." Thus came he, and so stayed, keeping, through many years, the larder full of game and fish. This wrinkled withered man went with them, paddling his birch slowly on, deep ladened with needed stuffs and precious things for dress and ornament at the marriage. For she said: "I will put on the raiment of my race when my foremothers reigned o'er half the world, and their banners, woven of cloth of gold, dark, with an emerald island at the centre, waved over ships which bore the trident at their bows, their sailors anchored under Mamelons a thousand and a thousand years before Spain sprang a mushroom from the old Iberian mold. I will stand or fall forever, Queen at Mamelons." So said she, and so meant. For all her blood thrilled with the haughty courage of that past, when fate was faced with open, steady eyes, and the god Death, that moderns tremble at, was met by men who gazed into his gloomy orbs with haughty stare as he came blackening on. So silently the silent man went on in his light bark, loaded with robes, heavy with flowered gold, woven of old in looms whose soft movements, going deftly to and fro, sound no more, leaving no ripple as it went, steered by his withered hands, down the black rivers of the north, toward feast or funeral under Mamelons.

CHAPTER V.

AT MAMELONS.

SUMMER was at its hottest. The woods, sweltering under heavy heat, sweat odors from every gummy pore. Flowers, unless water-rooted, withered on their stalks. The lumbering moose came to the streams and stayed. The hot hills drove him down. The feathered mothers of the streams led down their downy progeny to wider waters. The days were hot as ovens and the nights dew-less. The soft sky hardened and shone brazen from pole to pole. The poplar leaves shrank from their trembling twigs and the birches shriveled in the heat. But on the rivers the air was moist and cool, lily-sweetened, and above their heads, at night, the yellow stars swung in their courses like golden globes, large, soft, and round. So the two boats went on through lovely lakes, floating slowly down the flowing rivers without hap or hazard, till they came to the last portage, beyond which flowed the Stygian[1] river, whose gloomy tide flows out of death into bright life at Mamelons.

They took the shortest trail. Straight up it ran over the mighty ridge which downward slopes on the far side, eastward to that

[1] The waters of the Saguenay are unlike those of any other river known. They are a purple-brown, and, looked at en masse, are, to the eye, almost black. This peculiar color gives it a most gloomy and grewsome look, and serves to vastly deepen the profound impression its other peculiar characteristics make upon the mind.

strange bay men call Eternity. It was an old trail only ran by runners who ran for life and death when war blazed suddenly and tribes were summoned in hot haste to rally. But she was happy hearted, and, half jesting, half in earnest, said: "Take the short trail. My heart is like a bird flying long kept from home. Let me go straight." So on the trail the two men toiled all day, while she played with the sands upon the shore and crowned herself with lilies, saying: "The queens of my old line loved lilies. I will have lily at my throat when I am wed."

So, when night had come, the boats and all their lading were on the other side, and they were on the ridge, which sloped either way, the sunset at their backs, the gloomy gorge ahead. Then, pausing on the crest, swept to its rocks by rasping winds, the sunset at her back, the gloom before, she said: "Here will we bivouac. The sky is dewless, and the air is cool. The trail from this runs easy down. I would start with sunrise on my face toward Mamelons."

So was it done, and they made camp beneath the trees, a short walk from the ridge, where the great spruce stood thickly, and a spring boiled upward through the gravel, cold as ice.

The evening passed like a sweet song through dewy air. She was so full of health, so richly gifted, so happy in her heart, so nigh to wedded life with him she worshipped, that her soul was full of joyousness, as the lark's throat, soaring skyward, is of song. She chattered like a magpie in many tongues, translating rare old bits of foreign wit and ancient mirth with apt and laughable grimaces. Her face was mobile, rounding with jollity or lengthening with woe at will. She had the light foot and the pliant limb, the superb pose, abandon, and the languishing repose of her old race, whose princesses, with velvet feet, tinkling ankles, and forms voluptuous, lithe as snakes, danced before kings and won kingdoms with applause from those whom, by their wheeling, swaying, flashing beauty, they made wild. She danced the dances of the East, when dancing was a language and a worship, with pantomime so rare and eloquent that the pleased eye translated every motion, as the ear catches the quick speech. Then sang she the old songs of buried days, sad, wild, and sweet as love singing at death's door to memory and to hope; the song of joys departed and of joys to come. So passed the evening till the eastern stars, wheeling upward, stood in the zenith. Then with lingering lips she kissed her lover on the mouth, and on her couch of fragrant boughs fell fast asleep, forgetful of all things but life and love; murmuring softly in her happy dreams, "To-morrow night," and after a little space, again, "Sweet, sweet to-morrow!"

But all the long evening through, the old tongueless chief of measureless Mistassinni sat as an Indian sits when death is coming—back straightened, face motionless, and eyes fixed on vacancy. Not till the girl lay sleeping on the boughs did he stir muscle. Then he rose up, and with dilating nostrils tested the air, and his throat rattled. Then put his ear to earth, as man to wall, listening to the voices running through the framework of the world,[1] cast cones upon the dying brands, and, standing in the light made by the gummy rolls, said to the Trapper in dumb show: "The dead are moving. The earth cracks beneath the leaves. The old trail is filled with warriors hurrying eastward out of death. Their spears are slanted as when men fly.

[1] I have been often surprised at the many and strange sounds which may at times be heard by putting the ear flat to the sod or to the bark of trees. Even the sides of rocks are not dumb, but often resonant with noises — of running waters, probably — deep within. It would seem that every formation of matter had, in some degree, the characteristics of a whispering gallery, and that, were our ears only acute enough, we might hear all sounds moving in the world.

They wave us downward toward the river. Call her you love from dreamland and let us go."

To which the Trapper, answering, signed:

"Chief, old age is on you, and the memory of old fights. 'Tis always so with you red men.[1] The old fields stir you, and here upon this ridge we fought your fight of rescue. God! what a rush we made! The air was full of hatchets as of acorns under shaken oaks when I burst through. I kicked an old skull under moss as we halted here, that she might not see it. It lies under that yellow tuft. I have ears, and I tell you nothing

[1] It is said that Indians cannot sleep upon a battle-field, however old, because of superstitious fear. They admit themselves that it is not well to do it, and always, under one excuse or another, avoid doing so.

stirs. It is your superstition, chief. Neither living nor dead have passed to-night. A man without cross knows better. I will wait here till dawn. She said 'I would see sunrise in my face when I start for Mamelons,' and she shall. I have said."

To this the chief, after pause, signed back: "I have stood the test, and from the burning stake went beyond flesh. I have seen the dead, and know them. I say the dead have passed to-night. Even as she danced her happy dances, and you laughed, I saw them crowd the ridge and come, filing downward. They fled with slanted spears. You know the sign. It was a warning, and for us and her. For, with the rest, heading the line, there walked two chiefs whose bosoms bore the Tortoise sign. I knew them. They slanted spears at her, and waved us down; then glided on at speed. And others yet I saw, not of my race — a woman floating in the air, her mother, clothed as she shall be to-morrow, and with her a long line of faces, like to hers asleep, save eager looking, anxious; and they, too, waved us downward toward the river. This is no riddle, Trapper. It is plain. When do the dead move without cause? Awake your bride from dreams and come down. Some fate is flying with flat wings this way, I know not what. I only know the dead have waved me toward water, and I go."

So saying, he took the dark trail downward, and in the darkness disappeared.

"The spell is on him," muttered the Trapper, as he sodded the brands, "and naught may stop him. The old fool will do some stumbling on the trail before his moccasins touch sand." And saying this, he gently kissed the sleeping girl, and taking her small hand in his strong palm, he fell asleep; sleeping upon the crumbling edge of fate and death, not knowing. Had he but known! Then might wedding bells, not wail, have sounded over Mamelons.

. . . .

"*Awake! awake! my God, the fire is on us, Atla!*" so roared he, standing straight.

Up sprang she, quick as a flash, and stood in the red light by his side, cool, collected, while with swift, steady hands, she clothed herself for flight. Then swept with haughty glance the flaming ridge and said: "The light that lights my way to Mamelons, my love, is hotter than sunrise; but we may head it." Then, with him, turned, and fled with rapid, but sure, feet down the smoking trail.

The fire was that old one which burnt itself into the memories of men so it became a birthmark, and thus was handed down to generations.[1] None knew how kindled. It first flared westward of the shallow lake, where Mistassinni empties its brown waters from the north, and at the first flash flamed to the sky. It is a mystery to this day, for never did fire kindled in woods or grass run as it ran. It raced a race of death with

[1] It has been told me that many children born after the terrible conflagration that had swept the forest from west of Lake St. John to Chicoutimi, and which ran a course of 150 miles in less than seven hours, were marked, at birth, as with fire.

every living thing ahead of it, and won against the swiftest foot of man or moose. The whirring partridge, buzzing on for life, tumbled, featherless, a lump of singed, palpitating flesh, into the ashes. The eagle, circling a mile from earth, caught in the rising vortex of hot air, shrunk like a feather touched by heat, and, lessening as he dropped, reached earth a cinder. The living were cremated as they crouched in terror or fled screaming. The woods were hot as hell. Trees, wet mosses, sodden mold, brooks, springs, and even rivers, disappeared. Rocks cracked like cannon overcharged. The face of cliffs slid downward or fell off with crashes like split thunder. It was a fire as hot, as fierce, as those persistent flames which melt the solid core of the world.

Downward they raced in equal flight. Her foot was as the fawn's; his stride like that of moose. She bounded on. He swept along, o'er all. They spake no word save once. She slipped. He plucked her from the ground, and said: "Brave one, we'll win this race — speed on." She flashed a bright look back to him and flew faster. Thus, over boulders and round rocks, they sprang and ran. Above, the flying sheets of flame; behind, the red consuming line; around them, the horrid crackling of shriveling leaves; ahead, the water, nigh to which they were; when, suddenly, they ran into blinding smoke and lost the trail, and, tearing onward, without sight, she fell and, striking a sharp rock, lay still, numbed to weakness. The Trapper, stumbling after, fell prone beside her, but his strong frame stood the hard shock, and staggered upward. He felt for her, and found her limp. She knew his touch and murmured faintly, with clear tones: "Dear love, stay not for me: go on and live. Atla knows how to die."

He snatched her to his breast and through his teeth, "*O God! have you no mercy?*" then plunged onward, running slanting upward, for the smoke was thick below, and he knew the trees grew stunted on the cliffs. He ran like madman. A saint running out of hell might not run swifter. He was in hell, the hell of fire; with heaven, the heaven of cool, reviving water, just ahead. The strength of ten was in him, and it sent his body, with her body on his breast, onward like a ball. His hair crimped to the black roots of it. He felt it not. His skin blistered on cheek and hands. He only strained her closer to his bosom and tore on. With garments blazing, he whirled onward up the slope, streamed like a burning arrow along the ridge which edges the monstrous rock men call Cape Trinity, slid, tumbled, fell, down its smoking slope, until he came to where the awful front drops sheer; then, heaving up his huge frame, still clasping her sweet weight within strong arms, plunged, like a burnt log rolling out of fire, into the dark, deep, blessed tide.

. . . .

Morn came, but brought no sunrise. Smoke, black and dense, filled the great gorge, and hung pulseless over the charred mountains. Soot scummed the water levels, and new brooks, flowing in new channels, tasted like lye. Smells of a burnt world filled the air. The nose shrank from breath, and breathed expectant of offence. The fire brought death to ten thousand living things, and filled all the waste with stench of shallow graves, burnt skins, and smoldering bones.

The dead had saved the living, for the old chief lived. From the red beach he saw the Trapper's race for life along the smoking ridge, and paddled quick to where he made his awful, headlong plunge into Eternity.[1] From the deep depths he rose, like a dead fish to surface, his breath beaten out of him, but clasping still in tight arms the muffled

[1] The recess of water curving inward toward the mountains between Cape Trinity and Eternity is called Eternity Bay.

form. His tongueless savior — so paying life with life, the old debt wiped out at last — towed him to shore and on the beach revived him with rude skill persistent. He came to sense with violence, torn convulsively. His soul woke facing backward, living past life again. To feet he sprang at his first breath, and cried: "*Awake! awake! my God, the fire is on us, Atla!*" then plucked her from the sand where she lay, weak, as a wilted flower, and started with a bound to fly. The touch of her bent form, drooping in his arms, recalled his soul to sense, and he knew all, and reeled with the woe of it. Down at the water's edge he sank, cast covering cloth from head and hands, bathed her dark face, and murmured loving words to her still soul.

Through realms and spaces of deep trance

her spirit, lingering in dim void 'twixt life and death, heard love's call, and struggled back toward the shore of life and sense. From pulseless breast her soul clomb up, pushed the fringed lids apart, and gazed, through wide eyes of sweet surprise, upon his worshiped face: then sank, leaving a smile upon her lips, within the safe inclosure of deep sleep. All day she slept within his arms. All night she slumbered on. Wisely he waited, saying: "Sleep to the overtaxed means life. It is the only medicine, and sure. In sleep the wearied find new selves."

But when the second morning after starless night came to the world, she felt the waking gray of it upon her lids, and, stirring in his arms, like wounded bird in nest, moved mouth and opened eyes, and gazed slowly round, as seeking knowledge of place and time and circumstance. Then memory came, and she remembered all, and softly said, "Art thou alive, dear love? I have been with the dead. The dead were very kind, but oh, I missed you so," and with soft hand she stroked his face caressingly. The old chief mutely stood, watching, with gloomy eyes, the sad sight. He read the motion of her lips, and in his tongueless throat there grew a moan, and his dry lids wet themselves with tears. She noticed him and said: "You, too, alive, old servitor! The gods are strict, but merciful. Two of the three remain. The one alone must go. So is it well." Then to her worshiped one: "Dear love, this is a gloomy place. Let us go on. The smoke hides the bright world. I long for light. The fate is not yet sure. The blood of our old race holds tightly to last chance. We face it out with death to the last throb. Then yield, not sooner. Who knows? I may find sunrise yet at Mamelons."

So was it done.

They placed her on soft skins within the boat facing him who steered, for she said: "Dear love, the dead see not the living. If I go I may not see you evermore. So let me look on your dear face while yet I may. To-day is mine. To-morrow — I know not who may own to-morrow."

Thus, he at stern and she at stem, softly placed on the piled skins, her dark eyes on his face, they glided out of the deep bay, round the gray base of the dread cape that stands eternal, and floated downward with the black ebb toward the sea. Past islands and through channels intricate, they went in silence, until they came to where the Marguerite, with tuneful mouth, runs singing over shining sands, pouring out into dark Saguenay, as life pours into death; then breathed they freer airs, and the freshness of untainted winds fell sweetly down upon them from overhanging hills, and thus she spake:

"Dear love, I know not what may be. We mortals are not sure of anything. The end of sense is that of knowledge. We know we live forever. For so our pride compels, and some have seen the dead moving. But under what conditions we do live beyond, we know not. Hence hate I death. It is an interruption and a stoppage of plans and joys which work and flow in sequence; severs us from loved connections; for the certain gives us the uncertain, and in place of solid substantial facts forces us to build our future lives on the unfixed and changeful foundations of hopes and dreams. It is not moral state that puzzles. We of the old race never worried over that. For we knew if we were good enough to live here, and once, then we were good enough to live elsewhere and forever; but it was the nature of existence, its environment, and the connections growing out of these that filled the race whose child I am with dread and dole. For all the women of my race loved with great loves—the loves of lovers who sublimated life in loving, and knew no higher and no holier, nor cared to know. We cast all on that one chance; winning all in winning, and losing all if we lost. With me it is the same. I love you with a love that maketh life. I am a slave to it. It is my strength or weakness, as has been with the women of my blood from the beginning. I have no other creed, nor faith nor hope. To-day I see thee, and I have. To-morrow whom shall I see? The dead? I care not for the dead. There is not one among them I may love, for loving thee has cut me off from loving other one forever; unless the alchemy of death works back the creative process, undoing all of blood and nature, and sends us into nothingness, then brings us forth by new processes foreign to what we were, and wholly different from our old selves, which is a consummation horrible to think of."

"Nay, nay," exclaimed the Trapper. "Such cannot be. Our loves, if they be large and whole, grow with us, and with our lives live on forever."

"It may be so, dear love," replied the girl. "Love's prophecy should be true as sweet, or else your sacred books are vain. For in them it is written, 'Love is of God.' But oh, how shall I find thee in that other world? For wide and dim must stretch its spaces, and vast must be its intervals. This earth is small. We who live on it, few. Within the circle of three generations all living stand. But the dead are many. The sands of Mam-elons are not so numberless. They totalize the ages; the land they dwell in beyond mortal compass. Who may be sure of meeting any one in such a realm? At what point on its boundaries shall I wait and watch? How signal thee, by hand or voice, when out of earth, like feather, blown, by that strange movement men call death, into the endless distances, thou comest suddenly. Alas! alas! I know not if beyond this day, I, going out of this dear sunlight, may ever and forever look upon thy face again!"

"Atla," returned the Trapper, "I know not what may be. But this I know and swear, that if a trail pushed, seeking, through a thousand or ten thousand years, may bring me to thy side, we two shall meet in heaven."

"Oh, love, say those sweet words again," she cried. "Say more than them. Crowd into this one day, that I am sure of, the vows and loves of half a life, that I may go, if go I must, out of thy sight from Mamelons, heartful, upheld by an immortal hope. And here I pledge thee, by the Sacred Fire that burns forever, that if power bestowed by nature, or artfully acquired by patience working through ten thousand years, may find thee after death, then some time will I find my heaven in thy arms, not found till then. So, now, in holy covenant we will rest until we come to Mamelons, and ever after. I feel the breeze of wider water on my cheek, and breathe the salted air. I shall know soon if ever sunrise shine for me at Mamelons."

So went they down in silence with the tide that whirled itself in eddies toward the sea; past L'Anse a l'Eau, where now the salmon swim and spawn against their will,[1] past the

[1] At L'Anse a l'Eau, where the Saguenay steamers land passengers for Tadousac, the tourist will find a fine collection of large salmon at the upper end of the little bay or recess, for here is one of the salmon-hatching stations under government patronage.

sharp point of rounded rocks, where sportively the white whales[1] roll, and, steering straight across the harbor's mouth, where her Basque fathers anchored ships before the years of men,[2] ran boat ashore where the great ledge runs, sloping down from upper sand to water, and shining beach and gray rock meet.

But as they crossed the harbor's mouth,

[1] The white whales, commonly called porpoises, are very plentiful at the mouth of the Saguenay, and to a stranger present a very novel and entertaining spectacle tumbling in the black water. They are hunted by the natives for both their skins and oil.

[2] Personally, I hold to the opinion that the eastern hemisphere never lost its knowledge of the western, but that from immemorial times, the Basques and their Iberian ancestors visited at regular intervals the St. Lawrence, both gulf and river. Of course, the grounds on which I base such an opinion cannot be presented in this note.

sailing straight on abreast of Mamelons, its bright sands blackened and a shadow darkened on its front, and, as they bóre her tenderly to the terrace, where stood tent and priest, a tremor shook the quivering earth, and through the darkening air a wave of thunder rolled.

"Dear love," she said, "it may not be. The fate still holds. The doom works out its dole. I may not be thy wife this side grave. What rights I have beyond I shall know soon. For soon the sight[1] will come

[1] It is held by some that certain families have the power of "second sight," or to look into the future, come to them just before death. I have known cases where such power, apparently, did come to the dying. The Basque people held strongly to the belief that all of their kingly line were seers or prophets, and that, especially before dying, each had a full, clear view of the future.

to me, and what is hidden now will stand out plain." Then, lying on the skins, she gazed at Mamelons, looming vast and black in shadow, and, closing eyes, she prayed unto the gods, the earthborn, old-time fathers of her race.

But he could not have it so, and when prayer was ended said: "Atla, we have come far for marriage rite, and married we will be. Thou art mistaken. I have seen shadow settle and heard thunder roll before. In eye nor cheek are death's pale signals set. The holy man is here. Here ring and seal. Forget the doom, and let the words be read that bindeth to the grave."

To this she answering said: "Dear love, thou art in error, but thy word is law. My stay is brief. When yonder shadow passes I shall pass. There sleeps my father, and with him I must sleep. The earth is conscious. I am of those who were, earthborn, and so she feels our coming and our going as mother feels life and death of child. The sun is on the western hills. At sunset I shall die. But if it may stay up thy soul through the sad years, bid the good man go on."

Then took the priest his book, and, in the language of the Latins, so old to us, so new beside her tongue, whose literature was dead a thousand years before Rome was, began to bind, by the manufactured custom of modern men, whose binding is of law and not of love, and hence a mockery. But ere he came to that sweet fragment of love's law and faith, stolen from the past, the giving and receiving of a ring, symbol of eternity, she suddenly lifted hand and said:

"Have done! Have done! No need of marriage now. No need of rite, nor prayer, nor endless ring, nor seal of sacred sign. I see what is to be. The veil is lifted and I see beyond. I see the millions of my race lift over Mamelons. They come as come the seas toward shore, rolling in countless billows from central ocean. The old Iberian race, millions on millions, landscapes of moving forms, aligned with the horizon, come, marching on. Among them, lifted high, the gods. On thrones a thousand queens sit regnant, raimented like me. Their voice is as the sound of many waters:—

"'Last, best, and highest over all, we place thee.'

"The gods say so? So be it, then. Mother, I have kept charge. My love has won him.

The old race stops, but by no fault of mine. My people, this man is lord and king to me. See that ye bring him to my throne when he comes seeking to the West. Dear love, you will excuse me now. I must pass on; but passing on I leave my soul with thee. Make grave for me on Mamelons. Put lily at my throat, green boughs on breast, bright sand on boughs. Watch with me there one night. I will be there with thee. So keep with Atla holy tryst one night and only one — then go thy way. We two will have sweet meeting after many days." And saying this she put soft hand in his and died.

Her lover, kneeling by her couch, put face to her cold cheek, nor stirred. The holy man said softly holy prayer; while the old tongueless chief of Mistassinni wrapped head in blanket, and through the long night sat as one dead

Next day the silent man made silent grave on Mamelons. At sunset they brought her to it, raimented like a queen, and laid her body in bright sand; put lily at her throat, green boughs on peaceful breast, and slowly sifted clean sand over all.

That night a lonely man sat by a lonely grave, through the long watches keeping holy tryst. But when the sun came up, rising out of mists which whitened over Anticosti, he rose, and, standing with bared head, he said:

"Atla,[1] we two will have sweet meet-

[1] I named my heroine Atla, because I hold that the Basques not only are descendants of the old Iberians, but that the Iberians were a colony from Atlantis. I

ing after many days." Then went his way.

And there, on that high crest, whose sands

accept fully Ignatius Donelly's conclusions as to the actual old-time existence of a great island continent in the Atlantic Ocean, and believe that in it the human race began and developed a civilization inconceivably perfect and splendid, of which the Egyptian, Peruvian, Iberian, and Mexican were only colonial repetitions. Atla is, therefore, the proper name for the last of the old Basque-Iberian blood to have, as it is the root of Atlantis (Atla-ntis), the original motherland of all. I have never met Mr. Donelly, and may never meet him, and hence I make this opportunity to express the obligation I am under to him for entertainment and profit. The patience of the scholarship that could accumulate the material for a book like his "Atlantis" is worthy of a wider and more grateful acknowledgment than this superficial age of ours is able to give, for it cannot appreciate it. No man with any pretensions of scholarly attainments can afford to let "Atlantis" go unread.

first saw the sunrise of the world, when sang the stars of morning, beyond doom and fate, at last, the child of the old race, which lived in the beginning, sweetly sleeps at Mamelons.

UNGAVA

A COMPANION IDYL OF MAMELONS

To HER who has learned with me and from me the lore of woods and waters, the myths of ancient folk and the traditions of races now no more; who wrote the words here printed as my thought formed them and whose pleasure in the growing sentences made my pleasure in composing them; to whose faith and help I owe so much and of them may tell so little; to my adopted daughter,

F. Marguerita Murray,

as a tribute and testimony I inscribe UNGAVA.

THE AUTHOR.

BURLINGTON, VT., 1890.

CONTENTS.

UNGAVA.

A COMPANION IDYL OF MAMELONS.

CHAPTER I.

AFTER MAMELONS.[1]

THUS did the Doom of Mamelons work out its dole. And leaving in her grave the joy of all his life, the fairest, sweetest woman of her race, — whose women were the glory of the world, — down from the Mound of Fate the Trapper came with heavy step and

[1] Ungava is not in the true sense a sequel of "The Doom of Mamelons," for that tale stands complete in itself. Nevertheless, the two are closely connected, and structurally united in a close companionship, as two of the principal characters in Mamelons — the trapper

slow, as one who bears a burden greater than his strength, to where the tongueless Chief of Mistassinni stood beside his bark, his silent paddle in his hand, and to him slowly said:

"Old friend, in yonder sand my love lies dead. You helped me lay her lovely body down, where it must lie beyond the reach of loving hands forever. There, as she bade, I have kept holy tryst one night. She met me there. To that high crest where first the world was born, from silence and from starlight she came down and stood beside me. I saw her clothed in raiment like a queen,

and the old chief of Mistassinni—are leading ones in this story, and in it are necessarily many allusions which are more plain and enjoyable to the reader if he has previously read Mamelons.

and all her beauty riper grown stood stately in her form, and shone resplendent out of face and eye. She told me things to be. And, as she talked, I heard the stir of thousands round her, and through the starlit air above the sands approving murmurs run; but long and lonely stretch the years 'twixt this and hour of meeting. Empty are my arms of that warm life that should be nestling in them, and empty all the world. With eyes uplifted unto mine, upon my breast her mother died. The chief I loved is dead. And now she, too, is gone, and with her took in going all the sunshine of the world. You, now, and I are left alone. Two silent ones, for you are tongueless, and I with grief am dumb. We two are joined in brotherhood of woe. So in this bark of thine will you and I take seat, and you with silent blade shall steer it upward on the flooding tide of death-dark water,[1] colored like our grief, between the awful cliffs, which, leafless as our lives will be, have stood in dead, gray barrenness from the foundation of the world. So, now, old friend, from this dread shore of Fate push off, and we will go, I know not whither and I care not where. We two alone are left, and till death parts us will we bide together."

So was it done. Slowly, without word or

[1] The waters of the Saguenay are dark and gloomy to a degree unknown in any other river or body of water I have ever seen, and are noted, the world over, because of their peculiar sombre and sinister appearance. Looked at from above, they often seem to be as black as ink.

sign, the old chief lifted paddle and silently the light boat moved from that dread shore which for a thousand years had been the shore of fate, and through the whirling eddies, whirling strongly up and on the flooding waters black as their grief between the monstrous walls of rock the silent two went floating up into the silence of unknown hap and hazard.

All day they drifted on in silence, until they came to where the Marguerite flows crystal over shining sands. Then the dumb helmsman steered his light bark inward through the current, flowing swift and clear. With skilful stroke he pushed it upward through the eddying tide until he reached that lovely bend where silver birches grow, and where a spring pours down its wimpling line of liquid music, singing through the grasses, until it, laughing, runs into the smiling river. Then, standing on the strand, he to his stricken comrade said:[1]

[1] The reader must bear in mind that the language of pantomime, or sign language, has been brought to a wonderful perfection as a means of communicating thought among the Indians of this continent. The ancient Greeks, as is known to all scholars, found it adequate for the purpose of full dramatic expression, whether of comedy or tragedy. They did not originate it, but borrowed it from older races and ages. The reading of the motion of the lips is also an ancient accomplishment, if such a word is allowable in connection with such an art or practice. Nor is it nearly as difficult as one might imagine to follow the pantomimist, and catch the sense of even subtle shades of expression. Some have thought that it is the earliest, as it certainly is the most vivid and picturesque, method of imparting human thought.

"Listen, Trapper, to wisdom born of losses many and of many years. At Mamelons your love lies dead. Your thoughts are heavy and your heart is sore. The wounds of death are deep. Time is the only balm that heals its hurts, and change. These two salve all and heal at last, if ever. The island is no place for you or me. There sleeps her mother and there sleeps the chief. The house is empty as a nest when birds have flown and under snow the bough droops down. There will thy grief keep fresh and sore. Its ache will grow as grows thy sense of loss. Here will we camp to-night, and on the morrow northward will we go to far Ungava.[1] Upon its sands and

[1] Ungava is the name of a large bay which runs deeply into the body of the continent near the north-east corner of the Labrador peninsula. It is remarkable

ice, in distant years, I fought and hunted. There, perchance, I may find some, who, scarred in those old fights and gray, remember me. If not, it is the same. Among the Nasquapees is one who knoweth all. He can call up the dead.[1] His eyes see backward and before. There is but one thing I would know. It may be he can tell it me. Here will we sleep to-night. Perchance in sleep

because of its extraordinary tides, which rise to the height of sixty feet and more. Around it, formerly, the famous tribe of Nasquapee Indians — if they be Indians — had their home. Of these remarkable people I have spoken in my note concerning them in Mamelons.

[1] This is an allusion to a famous prophet or high priest of the tribe, who, apparently, was the last of a long line of prophets, who claimed to have powers such as the Witch of Endor possessed and exercised, when, if our Old Scriptures are to be credited, she called up the spirit of Samuel from the dead.

some dream[1] may come. If not forbid, to-morrow northward we will go."

To which the Trapper:

"Old Chief, your years are many and your words are wise. The wounds of death are deep, and time and change and God's sure help can only heal. The island is an empty nest. The fairest and the sweetest bird these northern woods may ever know, has flown. She has found summer land. She will come back no more. The island is the home of graves. Some things are there for me to do. But they can wait. His kinsmen watch the

[1] As is well known, the Indian is a firm believer in dreams as a method of mystic and valuable communication. From this old-time superstition no reasoning can turn him. He sincerely believes that the Great Spirit speaks directly to him in his sleep by their agency.

house, and they are true. When out of years I have, by many sights and deeds and varying haps, carved calmness, and been strengthened, I will go back. I will not go till then. I, too, have seen Ungava, and have fought upon its sands, and stumbled on its blocks of ice, blood-wet. I will go north with thee, and hear again the roaring of its tides, and hunt the seals beneath the fires that burn the end of the world.[1] It may be that in action swift my soul will find its rest, and out of changeful chance forgetfulness will come, and scab the gash of grief now bleeding red, and scar it to dull pain. We

[1] The northern Indians will gravely inform you that what we call the Aurora Borealis, or Northern Lights, are the reflection of flames which ever and anon rush out from the end of the world, which they hold to be forever in a state of combustion.

will go north, and bide together till we die." So was it done.

So went they northward, and for half a year did widely roam. Strange fortunes fell to them. They passed the sources of the streams that flow toward the south. They saw the forests dwindle down until the mighty pine was but a shrub. They visited old fields, where, in forgotten years old fights had been, whose only record was scattered and white bones. They made them bags of eider,[1] and housed themselves in snow. They trapped them furs which gave them garments such as princes wear. They fed on meat of fish and fowl and animal, juicy and fat, cooked with a hunter's art. For bread they digged them roots, which,

[1] The Nasquapee Indians sleep in bags lined with eider-down.

deftly parched and pounded, yielded substance sweeter than the wheaten loaf. So roamed they through the north, through those wild wastes where trails are scarce as honor among men. One, seeking day and chance, if they still waited; the other, balm for wounds within, and that forgetfulness which dulls the edge of pain and makes it easier to be borne. So leisurely they drew their trail into the north as men who seek at random, or seek forgetfulness of selves:—that sweet oblivion or dim memory of woes.

So roamed they on. One night they camped beneath a hill, one of a range that stretched a hundred miles from east to west: a ridge of mighty bowlders, meteoric stones and rocks volcanic, treeless, soilless, a monstrous jumble of chaotic débris that might be monument above a ruined world.[1] There in wild labyrinth of desolation they made their bivouac. Before they slept, the old chief, standing in the camp-light, signed:

"Trapper, some evil fate is coming swift as death. Twice on the trail to-day I felt the ledges shake.[2] I hear the sound of running noises under ground. The fire to-night

[1] Nothing can be imagined more desolate and dismal than this section of the Labrador peninsula. If Ignatius Donnelly's theory is correct, that a comet once struck the earth near what is now the northern extremity of the globe, one might easily imagine that, west and north of Ungava, he was standing amid the ruins caused by the awful catastrophe.

[2] Earthquake shocks are not infrequent throughout this section. Some years the seismic disturbances are felt for months together, and scarcely a year passes that one or more shocks are not experienced.

burned blue, and talked. I smell a storm.[1] This is a wilderness of rocks. There is no trail. If sun should fail what eye might thread a passage through? I fear some fate is coming. What counsel do you give?"

To which the Trapper made reply:

"Chief, lie down and sleep. The stars are bright. The sky is blue. No storm is coming. If it comes, we will bide in our bags. Two days at most will blow it out. Our food will last till sun comes forth. The rocks are

[1] Even many white hunters I have met in my wanderings have boldly claimed that the coming of great atmospheric disturbances was plainly interpreted by the nose. May it not be possible that the organs of smell, like those of sight, are much more acute in those who are "lone hermits of untainted woods" than in us who live from day of birth in smoky and foul atmospheres?

jumbled, and all look alike. Who cares? We are not boys. Can you and I lose trail? That were a joke. Your nose is not a hound's. No storm is coming. Lie down and sleep. Let ledges shake. Unless they shake me out of bag, I will sleep on." So spake he lightly, and, muttering in his throat, the old chief crept into his eider nest, and, like a duck within its warmth of feathers the two men slept.

That night the dreaded storm came down and such a storm no man had ever seen in all the North. Nine days it blew. Nine nights its roar was on the hills of rocks piled high as broken trees. Nine sunless mornings came. The falling fleece turned darkest night to gray. From out the north chaotic whirlwinds rushed, whirling in screaming eddies onward. The upper stillness, which, woven by the gods in silent looms, is folded like a downy mantle round the world as vestment cast by slumber over weary beds, was torn in shrieking shreds and blown down the gale in strips of noise. The forest, like a man entombed alive, moaned, writhed, and roared, unseen. Hills into distance ran from sight. The streams stopped running and the lakes lay shivering, dumb and black, beneath the ice that was itself invisible. The world turned gray, and through the whirling, eddying fleece the lenses of the eye reflected only falling flakes. Chaos had come again and all the earth was without form and void.

Amid the storm whose fury blotted out the world, the two men, blinded, faint from hunger, wandered on. Each day they groped for shelter; each night, burrowed under snow, awaiting death. All skill was vain; all courage useless. They felt that they were doomed. Twice had the chief refused to move. Twice had he fixed his eyes on vacancy. And twice the death-song struggled in his tongueless throat. The Trapper would not yield. His heart was true as tested steel to bravest hand. It would not break nor bow to shock, however heavy. Twice had he rallied his old friend from trance for further effort, when, staggering onward round the sharp edge of a ledge, they slipped together and both fell through covering snow into a fissure yawning wide, and downward half a hundred feet they slid into a mighty cavern!

So, into shelter under ground, through God's mercy, had they dropped, when, blinded by the storm, and hunger-faint, they stumbled from the cliff and fell. The cliff, a rounded bowlder nicely poised, had lost its balance as they fell, and, rolling after, lay on the shute through which they slid, huge and heavy as a hill.

Then spake the Trapper, as he staggered to his feet, grimly jesting in the face of death:

"Here are we safely housed, old friend, at last! Never did mongrel cur, chased by she-wolf, skurry into kennel faster. I fell with legs so wide apart that all the hillside followed. Its cobbles pelted on my back as I slid downward. I'll strike a light and see if we have host to welcome lodgers."

Then he struck light and to the wick of a short candle placed it; and as it kindled into blaze he held it high above his head and in the light it gave the two men sought with earnest eyes the nature of the place, and whether it were home or grave.

It was an old-time cave. Home had it been and grave, for those whose deeds and death are prehistoric. In ages lost to memory of men, man had been there before. Fleeing from sudden heat that blasted, or dreadful cold succeeding heat, or from that awful monster[1]

[1] Many tribes of Red Men have among them the legend of a great catastrophe caused by a comet striking the earth. The story or myth of a "flying dragon, breathing fire and smoke," is found in all old literatures, and always connected with a vast ruin wrought on the earth. There is no reason, in the nature of things, why a collision should not occur between the earth and one of the many "monstrous and lawless wanderers of the skies." Nor is it inconceivable that such a collision in the remote past did occur. Assuming this to be true, many remarkable and now mysterious phenomena on the earth's surface could be easily explained. Kepler de-

bursting out of distance into northern sky, nigh where the steadfast star now sentinels the heavens, and breathing fires in volume wider than the world, rushed, tearing downward toward the pole, struck the even earth head on and knocked it from its level poise, changing its course forever, so burying all in

clared that "comets are scattered through the heavens with as much profusion as fishes in the ocean." Lalande had a list of seven hundred comets observed in his time. Arago estimated that the comets belonging to the solar system, within the orbit of Neptune, number seventeen and a half *millions*. While Lambert says *five hundred millions* are a very moderate estimate. And this, be it remembered, does not include those that are constantly pouring in from the infinite spaces beyond the limits of the solar system. When the multitude of the comets is considered, the wonder is, not that *one* has struck the earth, but rather that, if I may so speak, the earth has managed to dodge them at all!

ruin : — hither to this deep cavern had he with his children wildly run, and, screaming, plunged into it, as men to-day running out of fire with garments blazing plunge headlong into saving wells.

There had he lived, there fed his hunger, worshipped God, wrought with ·his hands — and died. For, scattered here and there, were instruments of stone : a hatchet, flint heads for spears, and arrows sharpened with laborious pains. Brands, too, were there, which once had glowed with fire for human need, — charred proofs of tribes and primal things, which any careless foot may spurn as worthless, and yet be older than the Pyramids. Amid the dust the foot disturbed were teeth of men and animals that lived in the forgotten ages. Searching through an inner passage, seeking outlet. the Trapper found a knife of bronze lying on the floor, its handle resting in the dusty outline of a human hand, and wondered if the breast that felt it last had been of priest or victim. Who might say? Who, who might ever tell the secrets of that dread place and symbol? Here, penned with death, for many days they groped and sat in gloom. At last the Trapper, feeling that death was nigh, said suddenly, "Old friend, our time to say farewell has come." Then, for the last time lighted he the feeble wick, and, as it warmed, the small flame slowly grew until it globed with yellow light the central gloom. Then rose the chief of Mistassinni, cast robe of fur aside, and, grim, gray and withered, stood forth to sight, and to the Trapper signed:

"Trapper, we die a death of shame. We

are not men. We are as hedgehogs in a hole, shut in by ice. Here shall we die and rot, and be no more forever, — never see light of day, nor breathe the upper air. I am a chief. Before the Esquimau tore out my tongue and ate it, my voice was heard in every battle fought through all the North, and where it sounded men knew Death was there, and shrank. Only the Chief[1] and you had fame so great. In feasts and dance, and when the stake[2] was struck, our names were linked together like three equal stars, and mothers of the Esquimaux hushed crying child with whispered mention of our awful fame. But

[1] Referring to the chief who was uncle to Atla. [See Mamelons.]

[2] The stake around which the war dance is danced, and into which each warrior strikes his hatchet, thus signifying his enlistment for the war.

dying here like starving hog in hole, I never more may see the lodges of my tribe[1] nor sit in council with the chiefs among whom I am greatest. The battle will be set, and he I hate will live. And younger men will never know my fame. Do for me one more deed, far better than that one you did for me upon the ridge above the Saguenay when you did save me from the Esquimaux, and prove your love again. Draw now thy knife, and place its point betwixt the ribs that are above my heart, that I may lean upon it and die as warrior dies in battle under foeman's knife, and not be smothered like a hog in hole."

[1] An Indian believes that if he is smothered underground, his spirit will remain buried with his body, and never reach the Spirit-land, viz., that he will miss the blessing of immortality.

And from his shrunken shoulders, haughtily, his blanket did he cast, and posed himself above the burning wick whose dying flame began to waver, that friendship might do for him the deed he prayed for.

Then said the Trapper, speaking through the failing flashes of the light:

"Never before, old Chief, did friend in dying ask deed of me I did not do. But this I may not. I may not redden knife of mine with thy old blood. I am a man without a cross,[1] and such a deed I am forbid. It is not fit. Your superstition is not true. Out of this cavern filled with old-time bones, we two will go at death into free air: thou to the lodges of thy tribe; I to her throne.[2]

[1] A pure-blooded white.

[2] Referring to his joining at death his beloved Atla,

Hunger has done its work, and we are weak. We will lie down and sleep as after battle, battle-tired. Sleeping, we soon shall pass to deeper sleep, and so to happy waking. Old friend, the light is going. Brief is our parting. Look. With this failing flash I give thee dying cheer, and bid thee long farewell." And with the word the light went out, and in the gloom of that old grave of prehistoric man the two men stood, lost to each other's sight forever.

who, in dying [see Mamelons], beheld herself elected by the gods to sit on the "last and highest throne of her old race."

CHAPTER II.

THE COMING OF UNGAVA.

SO stood the two in darkness and in silence, waiting death. The one with Indian patience grim and dumb; the other, brave, high-hearted, revolving many thoughts. When, suddenly, the pulseless air moved with vibrations. The awful silence grew sweetly vocal, and a voice, clear-toned as silver bell or flute, said, from afar:

"Who speaks of dying and of shameful death? Whose voice bids friend the long farewell, and gives him dying cheer? No death is here, nor dying. Ungava comes!" And in the distant gloom, far down the caverned corridor, shone out a star, pure white, intense, illuminating all, and in its dazzling radiance, clothed in white fur from head to foot, a wand within her hand uplifted high whose point burned unconsumed, with face of snow, and eyes and hair of night's jet hue, floating on as vision seen in dream, there came — a girl!

So in the white light stood the three, and on the one the two did gaze with eyes that grew with wonder. No greater change might there have been had angel of the Lord descended to that cave to summon dust and bone of dead humanity to glorious resurrection. Then, rallying from first shock of vast surprise, the Trapper awe-struck said:

"Shadow or substance. Spirit or flesh. I know not which, strange vision, but by the living God I know that never unto man in deeper need did he send saving angel. Who art thou, thou who bearest name of wildest shore on the round earth, and of what world? Speak message out, and tell thy tale; for whether I be quick or dead, I know not as I look on thee."

Then, clear as bell or flute in evening air of summer, came the words, filling all the cave with sweetness like a song sung by unseen singer:

"John Norton, thou art known to me, for I have seen thee when a thousand miles divided. Amid the smoke of battle have I seen thee move when death went with thee, step for step. Asleep, at night, beneath the pines or at the base of rocks in strange wild places in the woods, above thee, sleeping, have

I stood and warded evil from thee. Wild beasts and wilder men with nose of hunger and with eyes of hate, have I turned or frightened from thy couch, and in the morning thou didst wake refreshed and safe, as one who knows not he is guarded. I am a spirit. This mortal frame I use, but am not of it. I am thy angel. Before his face that is forever veiled, I stand forever pleading. For every soul born into flesh has guardian spirit. Thine am I, and I have come in hour of need to save. Great service do I thee. Great service must thou do in turn for me. Here hast thou wandered into realms where, mid the ruins of a world collapsed, the arts and mysteries of that ruined world live on.[1] My

[1] The prophet of the Nasquapee tribe or race — I incline to the view that they are originally of a different

soul is thine. Thy soul is mine. We two are knit forever. So much I tell thee now. The rest shall be revealed as time moves on. My grandsire, after flesh, is Prophet of the North. He, child of the White God. This old chief knows my line, and therefore me. At Mistassinni did that line begin. At Mistassinni will it end. For he and I must sleep where his and my ancestors sleep, in that old

racial stock than the red Indian — held that the world had been wrecked by a vast and far-reaching catastrophe, and his race — all save a small remnant — destroyed by it. He also held that that old race, thus destroyed, was the custodian of arts and powers, mysterious and potent on dead and living alike, and that these had been originally taught them by "the gods;" viz., superior beings, who had come from some other sphere, bringing with them knowledge and powers "too high for mortal minds." And that this fearful knowledge had been continued in his line, or caste, and was known to him.

cave where sound in constant council voices of the dead and spirit murmurings."[1]

Then to the chief she said:

"Old Chief, above thy head a hundred years

[1] There is at Mistassinni a celebrated cave, which is regarded by the Indians with the utmost reverence, awe, and fear. Not one of them will ever look at it to this day in passing. The reason of this profound feeling seems to be found in their superstitious conviction that, from remote time, their dead chiefs were buried in it, as were also their prophets or sorcerers. It seems to have been the sepulchre of ancient days and people, for it has not been so used for a long time. They believe that the spirits of the dead hold their councils there, and that ghostly debate is constantly going on within its great chamber. I cannot ascertain that any one has ever actually visited this celebrated cavern, or has any accurate knowledge of its size or appearance. All that is known of it is that it was once the place of sepulchre, and is regarded with utmost fear and veneration by all the tribes of the North.

have rolled. Look with the eyes of many days. Behold, the first and last am I. Thou knowest fate, and its old voice. For, when the first White God did'st come from out of sea in boat not built by man, and, on the beach all wet and foul with brine and sand, was found by thy old sire, who then was boy, the prophet of your tribe did say, 'When girl is born instead of boy, the White Gods die.' Last chief of Mistassinni, here amid the ancient dead, the daughter of the White Ones, doomed like thee to end the line of glory, brings life and gives thee greeting."

Then did the grim old Chief do mystic deed. There, standing naked to his waist, the Totem of his tribe in red upon his breast, he lifted hands of plainest pantomime. Thrice did he wheel the sun around the earth in stately motion. Then strung his bow, and from his quiver four arrows drew, and, breaking pointed heads, he shot the harmless bolts to south and north, to east and west. So saying, "Thy reign is one of peace, and over all the earth." Then from his head the horned band he took —that symbol of old sovereignty, older than earliest throne,[1]—and from his wrinkled neck

[1] Horns, as symbolic of power and sovereignty, are, literally, older than thrones. Like the Cross—the old-time symbol of joy and plenty—they run backward in time beyond all interrogation. When or how the symbolic significance first arose, no one may ascertain. If there was no other evidence, the horns of the bison on the head-band of an Indian chief—for none save chiefs of the highest rank can wear them—would prove that the red men of this continent belong to the primeval races. As the Trapper would say, "That is a sign that cannot lie!"

the string of savage claws,[1] won in chanceful battle with the polar bear whose lightest blow is death, — a necklace whose every pearl had come at risk of life, — and laid them at her feet. Then on his withered breast he signed the sacred sign, and in solemn pantomime took

[1] The string of bear's claws round the neck of a chief is the highest possible proof of his skill, courage, and rank, since every claw in the necklace must have been taken from a bear that he with his own hand — unassisted by any — had killed. When it is remembered that the Indian had no weapon save his arrows, his hatchet, and his spear, some idea of the strength and courage required to secure such savage trophies can be formed. It takes a man of supremest nerve and courage to face a grizzly or polar bear with a Winchester to-day. What, then, must be thought of the stout-heartedness of one who, alone, and armed only with such feeble weapons as the native Indian had, would bravely attack these monstrous animals? Verily, no braver race of men ever lived than the red Indian of this continent.

goblet filled with water and poured[1] it on the ground. Then stately stood, and signed:

"Child of the Gods that were as snow! Daughter of Power and Mystery! Queen of Spirit-Land, whose coming in the flesh before I died, and going with me to the grave, was told a hundred years ago when I was born! Ungava! I, Chief of ancient times, about to die, salute thee! For, the same Voice that spoke thy fate, above me, sleeping in my father's tent, did say, 'This boy, a chief to be—the last and greatest of his line—shall die in battle with his foe upon the sands of

[1] The Indians of the Labrador peninsula present to the student of their habits and customs the curious spectacle of being both Christian and pagan, and in an equal measure. They will receive absolution at the hands of the priest, and the next instant engage with equal sincerity in an act of superstitious worship.

wild Ungava, when from the White Gods shall be born a girl that bears its name.' So art thou known to me, and so I know my foe still lives, and day and chance will come. Trapper, 'tis well thy knife stayed in its sheath, for now I know I shall not die like hog in hole, but like a warrior on the bloody field, with sound of battle in my ears, my foe beside me, and the dead in heaps around. So, like a chief shall I take trail that leads me into Spirit-land."

Then, after pause, the Trapper spake :

"Ungava, such boastful words are vain, and vain this pantomime of worship. The light of heaven never will he see, nor foe, nor battle red. Here are we penned with death. Through veins that never shrank before, a chill creeps on, and all my frame is weakened of my power. If thou art able, lead me from this dreadful place filled with the smell of graves and dust of mouldered men, to where my eyes can see the sun once more and to my nostrils come the wind that bloweth strong and pure; and, whether thou be witch or woman, soul or flesh, a living sweetness or the mate of death, to me thou shalt be angel evermore."

So spake the Trapper with clear tones. To him Ungava listened as wanderer listens to sweet song sung by familiar voice through dewy air to him home-coming:—a song that tells of love and home and peaceful days that have been his, and shall be his again forever. Then to him said:

"Fear not. Thou shalt see sun again. Upon thy face shall blow the wind that bloweth strong and pure. I am the queen of under and of upper world. The earth is hollow, and its outer shell is cracked with passages like the ice. I know them all. They are blazed trails to me. At touch of mine they flame with light far brighter than the sun. I know the under ways, — a labyrinth of passages which are to others endless as those tangled circles where the wicked dead go wandering, vainly seeking end of doom and the warm light of upper world, whose loves and light they forfeited by evil deeds. Through these I will guide safely on to where my grandsire sits whose eyes have seen the coming and the going of three times fifty years; who knows the arts and mysteries of lost worlds and ages, and has power on dead and living. Nor fear the chill that bringeth death, nor that dread weakening which has shrivelled up the full-veined strength that in thy frame was born, that I have seen go forth in battle mightily, until I veiled my eyes in horror at the redness of thy path amid the bodies, even as my soul, admiring, leaped, glorying in thy power. Here in this vial, cut from crystal under pole, where, vibrant, quick with living sparks, glows that electric force which is of Him nor man nor spirit ever saw, who rules the universe he made, and is forever making by laws that work forever, — the great I AM, — is vital liquid, which, were you dying and one drop was laid upon your tongue, you would rise up strong as a giant. Thus with my finger, moistened with this living essence, I wet thy bloodless lips. And thine, old withered Chief; and bid ye follow me. Twice twenty leagues we go through warm and cold, this way and that, through crust of earth cracked into fissures when the fire-breathing Dragon [1] of the North, whose tail was wider than the world, struck it head on, until we come to where my grandsire waits to show us, ere he dies, things that were and things that are to be. Come on! Come on! I am thy angel, Trapper! Follow thou the light that burns because I will it! Follow me, and fear not! I am Ungava!"

[1] The breadth of the tail of the great comet of 1811, at its widest part, was nearly *fourteen millions of miles;* the length of it, *one hundred and sixteen millions of miles.* The earth, remember, is only seven thousand nine hundred and forty-five miles wide. If the tail of such a comet as that of 1811 should sweep over our globe, it would not be large enough to make a bullet-hole in it!

CHAPTER III.

UNGAVA'S LOVE.

"HERE are we come at last. Here, safely guided, I have brought you through the under ways of earth: — the cracks and fissures in her solid crust, made in the ages of forgotten time, when out of distances beyond her orbit fell the bolt of ruin[1] that did rive apart the underlying granite. Past lakes of boil-

[1] It is a remarkable fact, and extremely suggestive, that a belief existed among the Indian tribes of the American continent that the earth was once struck by a vast physical body coming suddenly and at tremendous speed out of space, which caused an enormous ruin. We find this legend or old-time faith among the Aztecs, the Pueblo Indians, the Mandans, the Dacotahs or Siouxs, the Chicasaws or Creeks, and all the many

ing water, hot with central[1] heat; on banks of rivers sulphur-edged and bottomed; past springs whose flames burn blue and white, yielding no smoke, and dreadful pits which vent the smothered fires where righteous ignorance believes are penned the damned; I, you

branches of the Algonquin family. With more or less difference in descriptive details, as would naturally be expected, the great fact is the same in each tribe or race. With this legend are blended other ones of cave life, and the loss and renewal of the seasons, of day and night, and of vast climatic changes which came to portions of the earth inhabited by their ancestors, as the result of this monstrous visitation. Back of all these legends in time, there must have been some fact as the originating cause. At least, so it would seem.

[1] It is well known that in many of the deep, subterranean passages of the earth, especially in sections of the earth's surface subject to earthquake forces, the waters are hot, and some of the springs are, literally, of boiling water.

have guided and brought safely on to sure retreat. Here, crystal, flow sweet waters. Here bread and meat await your hunger. On these piled skins and under eider blankets lighter than moonlit air, you can find blessed sleep. Eat, drink, and sleep. Fear not. Trapper, this light is of the day. The air you breathe has poured in currents past the stars. When food and sleep have made you strong again, Ungava will return, and taking hand in hers, will lead you up where you shall see the orb that lights the world, and hear beneath the cliffs the tides come roaring in. Old Chief, sleep well and long. You shall find foe and chance, and out of glorious battle go like warrior to your sires. Eat, drink, and rest, while from my chamber nigh I sing the song that bringeth sleep and pleasant dreams."

UNGAVA'S SONG.

I.

When men do sleep, their angels keep
  Love's watch where'er they be.
They plant or till, they sow or reap
  On mountain, plain, or sea.
They lose or win, they laugh or weep.
  Who knows which it may be?
Sleep, Trapper, sleep. Dream, Trapper, dream.
  There comes no harm to thee.

II.

Fair, fair is she, whose deep dark eyes
  Gaze fondly down on thee.
Warm, warm her heart. Beyond the skies
  She longing waits for thee.
Her bosom white, her eyes of night,
  Are waiting there for thee.
Sleep, Trapper, sleep. Dream, Trapper, dream,
  Of Heaven, and her, and — me!

III.

Mine, mine to keep. Hers, hers to have.
  So are we blessèd three.
Soul of my soul. Heart of her heart.
  I keep. She has. Ah, me!
The lots are drawn. The wheel stands still.
  I keep. She has. Ah, me!
Sleep, Trapper, sleep. Dream, Trapper, dream,
  Of Heaven, and her, and — me!

IV.

Before our birth our fates are fixed.
  How may they altered be?
Why murmur, then? Why hope or wish?
  Who can the end foresee?
If I lose life, I yet may find
  The life I lose for thee.
Sleep, Trapper, sleep. Dream, Trapper, dream,
  Of Heaven, and her, and — me!

V.

Sweet, sweet to one is duty done
    When heart is ruled by will.
Sweet, sweet to know, as days go on,
    That you preserve from ill.
I may not have, but I can keep.
    So let the wheel stand still.
Sleep, Trapper, sleep. Dream, Trapper, dream,
    Of Heaven, and her, and — me!

So slept they through long hours. Then, by the longing of her heart impelled, Ungava came to where the Trapper slept, eager to look upon his face again. So softly to his chamber did she steal, and standing over him still slumbering on, she said:

"He sleeps! O sleep, rest lightly on him as the fur upon the sleeping ermine, when under its warm whiteness his little life reposes undisturbed. Be to his wearied frame as the cool water to the runner's feet, when, hot and swollen, they have brought him safely to the end of perilous trail, foe-chased. Be to his soul as is that volatile oblivion with which the gods ease pain, to wounded warrior, that he may feel no more the wounds of grief, the pain of bruises got in fearful falls, or have his dreams disturbed by roar of dubious battle. O sleep! sweet jailer of the soul, lock up his senses tight within his mighty breast; stop ear so closely that no vagrant sound may steal into its vaulted vestibule and beat its vibrant drum. Seal down his heavy lids that no swift flash of light electric shall, with pointed lances, pry their edges open; that I may gaze upon him undisturbed and question his unconscious soul, that, as the ancient oracles with lips of stone, not knowing what they said nor sensing joy or doom, so it may speak of fate and tell me if I live or die. Thrice round him will I walk that he in sacred circles three may be enfolded. Thrice over him, recumbent, the dust of dim forgetfulness I sift, that, through its drifts oblivious, he may not wish to rise. So sleeps he deep and well. Ah, me! if to my senses there could come such blest oblivion!"

Long stood she then and gazed upon him as he lay asleep. Then walked away, hands clasped in doubt; returned, and, standing over him, exclaimed:

"Oh, heart within, be still! Rebellious bosom, cease, cease, to lift and sink tumultuous! Be as the level sea when ebb is ended and the flood is stayed. And ye, pale sisters, gentle spirits of the skies, in whose sweet loving is no trace of mortal passion, help me who am earth-born, but doomed to be unto this man, or god, — I know not which, — a guard and guide forever; to chill this mortal warmth within me into ice, lest love shall bring me woe and anguish evermore. Ah, me! Ah, me! That I, a woman, should be doomed to look upon a man, like this! To see his soul pure as a child's; the gentleness of his spirit when unvexed; the might of hand which, single and alone, shapes battle; the modesty of nature too humble to know its greatness; and that old sense of truth which sweareth to its hurt and changeth not, keeping word and bond to lowliest given unto edge of death, — and be forbid to love him! Did ever woman on the earth before have fate like this fall on her! Oh, thou who did'st weave fate for me, appear, appear, and tell the child of ancient days, if I do right or wrong to question destiny!"

Then, in reply, from out the gloom of farther distance came a voice, saying:

"Ungava, light of face but dark of soul,[1] fear not to question and to know. The Powers that work for thee are mighty. The threads that wove thy fate were mixed and tangled dubiously. Love cuts all knots, and love, perchance, may out of fate deliver. Child of the Past, the old gods love you, and behold. Call up his soul and question freely. It shall speak truth oracular, and to his breast return not knowing."

Then, rallying courage for the deed, Ungava said:

[1] Referring to her foreboding of coming doom

"So be it, then. I will call up his soul and know the truth. God! If from his soul, unconscious, I should learn that from his eyes one look of love would ever come to mine before I die! Such look would last me through eternity and make my heaven a memory!" Then, proudly posed, with hand extended, grasping wand of power, she sang:

"From out his breast where thou art hid,
Oh, soul, come forth when thou art bid.
Prepare to leave thy home of sense,
And love shall be thy recompense.
For one brief moment rise and tell
The fate that makes my heaven or hell.
I fain would know what will befall.
So come, and answer love's sweet call.

Now, by the mother that did bear,
By powers of earth and powers of air,

By that sweet thing you most do love,
On earth below or heaven above.
By babe in cradle, corpse in grave,
And by this wand I now do wave
Above his sleeping breast, arise,
And here take form before my eyes."

Then was such sight as mortal never saw. Around the Trapper, as he slumbered on, a smoke as that of incense did arise, in color rosy-red, until it hid his sleeping form from sight of gazer; and out of its enfolding came a voice, which said:

"I heard a voice I may not disobey call me from out this sleeping body that I animate and which to me is as strong hand to the directing will. Why am I called before my time? Ungava, what would'st thou know of me, or him?"

Then said Ungava:

"If ever I may have thee as mine own."

To which the Voice replied:

"Yea, I am thine already. We two belong to him."

Ungava:

"But I am woman. And a woman's wants are mine. Unless he loves, I must bear doom and dole. Oh, tell me, will he love me?"

To this the Voice:

"When in the cave which, but for thee, had been his grave, he swore—'If thou would'st lead him forth where he might see the sun and breathe the air of heaven, thou should'st be Angel to him evermore.'"

Ungava:

"I know. I know his angel will I be. But will he *love* me?"

Again the Voice:

"The woman that he loves must be a queen."

Ungava:

"Queen! Queen am I. My throne is ancient as the Stars of Morning. Earth and air, past world and future, rule I. Speak once again. Shall I be Queen to him?"

To this the Voice made slow and solemn answer:

"If thou would'st have him break his faith and be to word and bond untrue, living or dead, then may'st thou be his Queen."

Then slowly thin and thinner grew the smoke until it vanished, and in the chamber dim and dark Ungava stood above the Trapper, slumbering on.

"Break faith!" she slowly said. "To word

and bond, be, living or dead, untrue! Oh, soul, thou did'st mistake if thou did'st think a woman's love would tempt the man she loved to such a deed. This man is honest. Such other one there may not be to-day on earth. Within his breast honor is as the breath is to his nostrils. Who, by the gift of all her heart, has paid the price and owns him, I know not. What woman of these later days when women have lost ancient beauty and are dwarfed from loyalty's high port to fickleness, might with her little self pay queenly price, is past all credence. Nay, it must be false. Such woman lives not. The time has been when women in their beauty wedded gods, and immortality paid the price of death to win them, and winning them, died happy in their arms. But that is past. From some old grave of porphyry or pearl, where she in sweet embalmment slept, had he the power to summon up the beauteous dead of olden time, some Queen, crowned and raimented in royalty, with all the fire and passion of her sex's perfection in her blood, might have arisen at his call, and, seeing him in battle or on the edge of death stand fearless, flung herself into his arms and claimed him for herself and for her throne. But now! It cannot be. There is no woman living fit for him. My power shall seek and find her. He has been cheated. My eyes shall see. If she be fit for him—alas! alas! I yield him to her arms, and yielding him I will lie down and die, and in the grave find—perhaps—forgetfulness! But if she be not fit; if she stand dwarfed beside him; if he were cheated by some accident of fate that came with tardy foot or ran too swift; if she be not as crown to kingly head; then will I win him to myself, and so be perfect angel in being perfect woman. But hush! He moves! Ah, what a sigh was that! I thought I was the only one that sighed. I will away, and come again when he awake."

Then vanished she. As light retreats into the west at day's decline so glided she into the farther openings of the cave, still gazing backward as she faded into darker distance. The Trapper woke. His eyes moved in their sockets, seekingly, as one who, sleeping, has lost sense of place and time and circumstance; then memory came, and sitting half recumbent murmured he:

"Ungava! Atla! It was a dreadful dream!

As wild as chief e'er dreamed sleeping over-tired on some old battle plain. I will arise and wash my heated face with cooling water. I would I knew where water runs that might this dreadful dream wash from my memory!"

Then in the ice-cold tide that ran in pleasant murmurs down the cavern's side he bathed his heated face and cooled the fever in his eyes, and, thus refreshed, stood gazing downward musing — when suddenly he stooped, and with observant eye studied the cavern's floor, and said:

"By sacred[1] sign on rifle stock I swear that little imprint there was outlined by Ungava's

[1] Many of the rifles among the northern Indians and trappers, partly from priestly influence, perhaps, and partly from religious or superstitious motives personal to the owner, have the cross carved or painted on them.

foot! See! Heel and forefoot have left mark, but the arched interval between, too high and firm for weight to flatten, has left the dust unstirred. The savior of my life did stand and watch me as I slept! Aye, she with face like purest snow, and gloomy soul as it were ever under shadow, and eyes that hold within their fringes, jet as night, the sorrow of a world long dead, who out of old-time grave and instant death did snatch me, did watch and ward keep over me in sleeping. What may I ever do to balance up the scales that now so heavily slope obliquely in her favor? She said great service must I do for her. I, standing in that dreadful tomb, chilled and weakened nigh to death, did give her word and bond if she should lead me to the upper world where I might see the sun once more and feel the air blow strongly on my cheek, she should be angel to me evermore. That word and bond thus given will I keep if hand or heart of mine may keep it this side death, or on beyond it. But, God of heaven, what is this? That impress in the Polar fur where lay my head! If death were settling darkly in my eyes, through dying film and glaze well should I know that little trail. There stood Ungava. Here above my head did Atla stand. My God, that they, my savior and my Love, should in this chamber stand together over me, and I sleep on! Am I on earth, or spirit land?—What may this visitation mean?"

Then as he musing stood Ungava came with noiseless step into the chamber, and gliding to his side she gently said:

"Trapper, twice has the sun come to the

earth and gone since thou did'st sleep, and now the moon shines whitely on the world. If thou art rested, we will go and thou shalt look upon her beauty and shalt hear the music of the sea which rolls its rhythm under sounding cliffs. What troubles thee? Hath not thy sleep been sound and restful?"

"Sound, sound it was in truth, O thou whose face is as the moon, my savior and my angel: but, O Ungava, as I slept strange dreams did come!"

"Dreams?" said Ungava. "What dreams did vex thy sleep, may I not know?"

"Aye, aye," he cried, "thou shalt know all. For thou do'st love me and art wise beyond the wisdom of dull, earthly man. Perchance thou can'st the riddle read and tell me what the vision means."

Then calmly she: "Say on, and tell me all. No doubt I can the riddle read and give its meaning."

Then solemnly the Trapper said:

"Ungava, listen. As I lay, my senses locked in slumber deep, — so deep I doubt if roar of coming battle would have stirred me, — forgetful of all earthly happenings as the dead: suddenly I seemed to hear the sound of music coming through the air in strangest song by dead or living heard, — a song sung for my soul! In answer to that song my soul did leave my bosom and slowly rising stand, as a thing unseen, above me. Then voices did I hear. Questions that my ears could not retain were asked and answered. Some soul was seeking of my soul for knowledge which it would or could not give; and all the world around me was as are the heavens when the clouds above Ungava's torrent tides at sunrise roll upward rosy red. Then, suddenly, the voices ceased; my soul sank downward to its mortal home within my breast; the red clouds faded, and I knew no more until I woke. Spirit of knowledge, tell me what it was I heard or seemed to hear. What is the meaning of this dreadful dream?"

Then said she, lightly, "Dear friend, thou wast o'er-tired. Thy body had been sorely taxed, and all thy senses tumbled into sleep as shot bear tumbles over edge of cliff and at the base dies struggling. It was a fever vision, an unreal distortion of the fancy; nothing more. Forget it."

Then did the Trapper, strongly moved, place hand upon her shoulder, and exclaim:

"Ungava, I can see some dread is on thee, and from fear of hurting me thou holdest back the truth. Thy soul is wiser than thy words. Look at that imprint in the film of dust upon the floor. There did my body lie. There at my feet thy foot did come and stand. Were I on dying bed, with dying gasp I'd swear that thy white moccasin did'st make that imprint on the floor. That is not all. Angel of my life! Savior in hour of death! Look here, here in the snowy fur of this white polar's skin, see! see that footprint where a little foot did leave its tell-tale outline in the yielding hair! Whose foot made that? There at my feet, Ungava, as I slept, did'st thou or thine own spirit stand. And here, by Him who made the world, were I at judgment bar, with hell before me, I would swear, upon this skin, seen or unseen by you, with arms outstretched above to shield or claim, did my sweet Atla stand! My God! what does it mean?"

Whiter than winding sheet her face beside his, gazing, grew. One hand clutched breast as if to tear it open. Back from her shoulder stretched her other arm, rigid and stiff. The hand was clinched in horror. Her widely opened eyes bulged wildly prominent—two orbs of black surprise. Then into air her white hands did she dash, and such a scream burst out of mouth as never shredded air before. And hurling wand from quivering hand, she dashed from out the chamber as if upon her had come down, like bolt from heaven, an overwhelming fear or shame.

CHAPTER IV.

THE WIZARD OF THE NORTH.

IN his vast chamber, vaulted high, whose ledge-like sides were knobbed with metals, precious stones, gold, silver pale, pyrites of iron, garnets, blocked crystals, diamonds barbaric, stones of blood and countless gems, and from whose dome stalactites pendent hung, sat the Great Wizard of the North. This caverned hall was Nature's marvel. It was as if some god before first day and night had been, when chaos ruled, and all the globe was soft as heated mud, with hands whose palms were wide as landscapes, had in wildest freak or wanton merriment, with strength gigantic, flung all metals known to forming nature down in showers, and laughed to see them fall into the stiffening ooze, which, hardening, held fast the treasure-trove of mighty mirth. Thus, when the cavern was by shock volcanic formed, its sides and vaulted roof wide-spanned and high were weighted with the wealth of empires. In this vast chamber thus adorned, rich in barbaric splendor, the Wizard of the North, her grandsire, Ancient of Days, whose stay on earth was thrice the length of mortal man's, sat in his awful chair — a seat of power which had come down from primal days, huge and high, carved with weird shapes, bristling with polished horns whose every point shone like a star — on jet-black pavement placed, upon whose lustrous gloom was traced in gold the sacred circle of the

Zodiac. His hair was white as whitened wool. His face was pale with years and thought and study of deep things. His eyes were living blackness. Above them brows of snow projected. On one thin hand there shone such stone as never man beheld, which flashed and glowed, changed color fitfully, then veiled its splendor in dull red, and slept. Anon its mystic fires would blaze again, and hot and hotter burn until they flamed the hand with splendor. Within the other hand, laid listless on his lap, was rod of that old mystic metal which to our modern ignorance is but a name, but once, with its strange powers, was known to men and had high use. In it were noises constant, as of snapping fire, and ever now and then a spark shot forth. Nor lacked it power to move and lift the hand that held it.

It was strange rod. A living proof of ancient mystery which startled Egypt into justice, if sacred text be true.[1] Thus, in strange state and style, the mighty Wizard of the North, the weird embodiment of powers and arts and vital agencies beyond the ken of moderns, sat musing, lost within himself. Then opened he his mouth and, as one holding audience with himself, he said:

"I know not what it means! Thrice has the Rod stood upward in my listless palm, unmoved by me! Not for a hundred years has this old symbol on my hand, instinct with primal sense, burned with such fierce

[1] Exodus, vii. chap. 10, 11, 12.—"And Aaron cast down his rod before Pharaoh and before his servants, and it became a serpent. Then the magicians of Egypt cast down every man his rod, and they became serpents; but Aaron's rod swallowed up their rods."

and fitful fires. Twice past me since I sat within this chair my ears have caught the sound of flitting feet. They came in haste, and when they went, they flew. I felt, but could not see the presence pass. It must be so. One of that race which planted earth with power and beauty and high knowledge has drawn a line across the distances, so vast that light itself might never shaft the mighty intervals, and in this cave has come and gone! There is not other one unless of that one race, in living-land or dead-land, my eyes might not behold in passing. Nor, of that race is one, unless she be of that old queenly line that lifted gods unto their throne, and by that graciousness did make them greater. But wherefore? What is there here for them or one of them, that she should leave her throne, which, were its glory tenfold brighter than the sun's, is yet so far removed from this small earth that not a point of light might tell its place or glory to a mortal's eye? What soul is here which through such space could send or call forth message? The chief of Mistassinni, withered and old, sleeps out of weakness unto strength, waiting for foe and chance. The Trapper, a vital man and primal in the greatness of his nature, but humble, and content with chase and hound and honest fight and mortal circumstance, sleeps to the music of the falling rill, lulled into slumber by Ungava's song. She, under fate to serve him, as higher spirit lower, caught in the eddy of a mortal passion, spins struggling round, and wildly seeks to know the issue ere it comes. These three are here. No more. Why should a mighty throne in distant universe be moved by what is here, to visit, invisible, this earthly cavern? There lifts the Rod again! The Ring burns hot as fire! What means it? Hist! I hear the stroke of flying feet and rush of garments. It is. It is. Ungava flying comes!"

Thus from the chamber and his presence fled she terror-stricken, filled with shame, that she had been observed by one unseen of her when she revealed her soul to his, seeking to know her destiny. Wild with fear she fled as flees the fawn, when by his yell the springing panther is revealed, — a ball of tawny fury falling through the air, above it feeding. So she with flashing feet fled fast, her garments streaming as streams the plumage of a pheasant sailing on, until she came to that high hall where, in his chair of mystic state, there sat the Wizard of the North, her grandsire, pondering on ancient things and signs that stirred his soul. Into his awful presence wildly did she burst, and with white face and hand high lifted, before him stood and cried:

"Sire of my sire, Ancient of Days, who hath the early and lost knowledge[1] of the

[1] It is by no means improbable that, as the great prophets, seers, sorcerers, or wizards — call them what you please — of all peoples and times have claimed, there was in the beginning of the world a far closer connection between this earth and the invisible worlds, than now is provable. In all sacred literatures, whether Christian, Jewish, or Pagan, — so called by us whose pride is equalled only by our ignorance of primal things, — this claim is boldly made, and miracle-working, or the doing of things outside the regular course or order of nature, is made, in them all, the very basis of the

world and all its power on dead and living, tell me, thou who taught me mystery and armed my hand with Rod of power and to my lips gave incantations that out of ashes of old urns and dust of ancient graves can call forth those who once with life did warm the mouldered clay, and from the bosom of the

structure around which they, as the verbal expression, have grown. It is evident to all scholars that back of what is known as modern civilization were other and more perfect ones, whose very ruins are a marvel to us all. It would seem that as we are only mere copyists in architecture, so we are only borrowers from the past of all that is really valuable in our faiths and moral code. No one with a heart can but lament that there is to-day no connection, whatever, in the form of communication, between those who live on the earth and our loved ones who live beyond it. The great loss that has fallen on man is this entire loss of the old-time connection with the invisible world.

living summon the soul articulate, and to my eyes didst give the sight which sees through space and graves: tell me, if in the universe there moves a body or a soul that, coming out of living-land or dead-land, can stand within arm's reach of me and not be seen?" So cried she standing in her fright before him.

Then he in answer:

"Ungava, daughter, last of my race, born unto dubious doom, to whom I have revealed the mysteries of life and death, and taught those ancient arts which give to lip and hand an awful power, and to thine eyes the sight that looketh, seeing, into graves and far beyond; what has disturbed thy soul? What power has baffled? Tell me plainly all, that I may plainly answer."

Then she in haste, awe-stricken, made reply:

"The Trapper slept. I am a woman and I love him. The threads of fate spun at my birth are tangled with his own. If he shall love me, happy will my life go on and happy will it end. I then shall be as mortal woman having lived and loved. My children will come after and our race be endless. If not, I do lose all that earth holds for a woman, and I die unmated, and in loneliness I shall live on forever. The rill with soothing murmurs fell. I sang him soothing song. He slept. Above him sifted I the dust which brings oblivion to mortal sense. Then from his breast I summoned forth his soul and questioned it if it might tell me, if my destiny were joy or woe. His soul obeyed me and made answer as I asked. I went. He woke. I came again. He was disturbed in soul. My spell was almost broken by some other spell. Some other power, most potent, had almost, by a dream, betrayed me. I was amazed, but passed it lightly off. In vain, for, in the dust where I had stood he pointed to my footprints, and did say, 'There didst thou or thy spirit stand as I lay slumbering.' Then to another footprint plainly pressed into the yielding fur of the white skin on which his head was laid, he pointed, and exclaimed, 'Here, with arms outstretched above my head to shield or save, did my own Atla stand.'

"Sire of my sire, great Seer and Prophet, who is this Atla? What spirit is there in the universe more strong than I, when standing,

Rod in hand, in incantation? Tell me, by Ring and Rod, if one there is in living-land or dead-land that can stand within arm's reach of me at such a moment, seeing, and remain unseen by me?"

Long sat he without speech. The Rod moved in his hand and from the Ring there blazed a flash of conscious flame. His eyes were fixed upon her startled face. Slowly and soundless moved his lips. At last he murmured, as murmuring to his soul:

"Atla? Atla? Atla-ntis![1] Is, then, the

[1] This refers to the belief of many scholars and those who have thoughtfully, with learned minds, examined the subject first broached by Plato, that in the Atlantic Ocean, stretching westward from the coast of Africa, was a great continent-island called Atlantis, from which the Atlantic Ocean derived its name, and that in this island the human race began its career.

old race gone from earth they loved and ruled, forever? Is that first tree of knowledge stripped to its last sweet leaf? It must be so. How did it read? Alas! How many years and graves have sifted down their smothering dust upon that sentence since 'twas said. Can I recall it? Aye, now it comes. '*The last and best shall bear the name of Motherland.*' Atla, the last of that great queenly line, is dead, and with her died her race. Ungava lives, and with her lives her race,—perhaps. Now see I all. Now read I well the riddle. '*Love cuts all knots, and love may out of fate deliver.*' If he may love her?"

Then to Ungava plainly did he say:

"Ungava, daughter, listen. I now will tell you gravest things. We must take deepest council. In the beginning two races were on earth, the earth-born and the visitant. In union were they joined and from the union two other races sprang. Ours was not greatest. The other greater was. It held the cradle of the world, and hence, prolific, sent its children toward the setting sun and southward. Our race the other was, and we came northward, which then was Summer-Land. Thus separate, divided, each of the two held to its own development in power and rank. Ours was the lesser, always. They built on reason and present things. We on the future world, credulous and superstitious ever. This Atla is the last and greatest of that race and its old queenly line, as thou art last of that religious Caste with us, that holdeth Rod and Ring of power. By some strange chance she must have met this Trapper, and have loved.

From distance greater than the farthest star from earth a thousand times, as you did summon forth his soul to claim it, she, hastening hither, flew. I heard her come and go, invisible to eyes to which all graves are only mirrors. This Rod did lift and bow obedient as she passed, and on my trembling hand the conscious Ring flashed startled recognition. She, she it was who stood above the Trapper's head, unseen of you. Greater than we, she is. Her power is stronger. Ungava, Atla is your rival, and she knows all!"

Then stood she white in dumb amaze at what her ears had heard. Atla her rival, and Atla had seen all! Who was this Atla? Where was she and where was she not? Perhaps e'en now her mighty orbs were on her! What might she do?

Then to her, standing thus all white with fear, her grandsire came. He took her hand and gravely said:

"My daughter, child of a race that dieth with thee if thou diest without issue, on yonder couch of skins I pray thee seek some needed rest. Thou art o'er-taxed. This matter leave to me. It needs grave thought and deepest wisdom, lest by blunder we lose all. Sleep thou in peace. I will the Trapper summon here and tell him much of ancient times and things. I will observe his soul, and at the last lead up to thee. Such man as he was never on this earth, if, seeing thee as he shall see, knowing thee as he shall know, his soul shall not in love or pity give itself to thee. So on this couch convenient let now thy frame repose. Close eyes; yield mind and thought to me. While with entreating and persuasive gesture I from thy soul draw trouble and call sweet slumber down. So, gently does she pass from ills that are and thoughts of ills to be into that realm that lies beyond the line of mortal sense and pain. I would that when she wakes she might awake into a world of equal peace."

CHAPTER V.

THE CONJURER'S ACCOUNT OF THE GENESIS[1] OF THE WORLD.

"HERE have I brought you, Trapper, that, in answer to your questioning, I might narrate the Genesis of the world, and tell you of the races which earliest dwelt on earth; of that first innocence which represented God,

[1] Whatever the reader may think of this as an accurate history of the beginning of the world and the "Fall of Man," it can doubtless be regarded as accurate as, and certainly more philosophic than, the one to which Milton stands sponsor in his "Paradise Lost;" that magnificent fiction of imagination, which has imposed a theology upon the Christian world which for the most part is diametrically opposed to good sense and sound Scripture both.

and how it fell; of arts and powers once known, now lost to men, and of that primal truth which underlies religions, superstitions, creeds, and is to them what vital element is to human blood. Here sit thou down, and, while Ungava sleeps, I will rehearse the tale of olden times, and you shall know the lore of that old world which is forever gone and all the glory of that race which once shone on the heads of millions, but which, like candle burnt to socket, now flickers feebly in two feeble lives. Never before, beyond the limits of our Caste did this old lore go forth; but you shall know the truth as it has come from mouth to mouth in sacred speech and accurate, from those who saw and knew whereof they told. I tell you, hoping it may live when she and I are numbered with the stars.

"This, then, was in the beginning, and this the cause and order of that first development whose ruined glory is to-day a marvel.

"No art or science, Trapper, worth the name was ever born on earth. All have come down from races throned amid the spheres, who, through unnumbered ages, had clomb slowly up the slopes of fine intelligence, and terraced Heaven with knowledge. When these on wing inquisitive in downward flight came to the earth, with them they brought all knowledge and all grace, and planted here the germs of needed progress. By these the earth in infancy was taught. Knowledge was borrowed from the skies. The seeds of every precious growth were sown widecast from hands whose skill eternity had taught. Through these superior ones the earth did gain and lose all worth the having. From them it gained the skill to build, to fashion, and to mould; and traces of their mighty work are found to-day in ruins wide as acres, in forms that stand gigantic in the forests of the East, in jungles which once were gardens of the gods, in mountains disrupted by volcanic shocks, but which, smooth-sloped and joined by intervals of verdure, once gave summer residence to those who longed to breathe the cooler airs from snowy summits blown, that are a wonder. Men stand and gaze at them astounded, not knowing what hand or skill could shape and hew such mighty sculptures. From them, too, came the knowledge of the skies. They were the Stars of Morning who sang the heavens into place and named to human ears the constellations. They fixed the orbit of the earth; called time from out eternity by measurement of day and night, of months and years; and zoned the earth by temperatures. They did unfold the mystery of the magnet circle around which sweeps the restless steel, and so gave courage unto men to push their ships beyond the sight of land, sail far and wide through pathless oceans, bravely trusting life and gold to a sliver of thin metal, thus giving birth to commerce which stands parent to the brotherhood of man. From them, too, came the arts of healing; the use of poisons, which, left untouched till time of need, are antidotes to death; the knowledge of all herbs medicinal, which give to every pain and ache its healing leaf; of oils, which, penetrating joint and bone, drive out the lurking pain, or, spread as ointment on the skin, pink it with health and smooth all wrinkles out, — those scars of smiting fortune; of perfumes, how distilled, how mingled, how preserved, that out of many sweets perfected sweets may come, that mortals might be charmed from joys of grosser to those of finer senses. From them, moreover, knowledge came of metals, where found, how worked and manufactured into forms of use and ornament according to the laws of high utility and taste. They taught the laws of architecture unto men; the principle of the arch, — that key of utmost strength; the column, plain or fluted, — that symbol of high stateliness; the crowning capital which flowers the stony stalk with airy beauty; and how tall tower and minaret and steeple and the rounded dome should shape the massive structure underneath into proportions rhythmic. The cereals that give food to man were from the wild abundance of material chosen and by careful culture propagated unto perfection. Last of all, they taught them written language, symbolic and phonetic both. First in pictures,[1] that their childish eyes might be enticed to learn and easily catch sense from shade of color and from shape. Then in arbitrary forms which were for scholars, ranges of high thought and universal traffic in ideas answering universal needs; that all the race, in all its tribes and families, in every zone remote and clime distinct, might by one universal avenue come at last, as after tri-

[1] Probably the oldest language or method of communicating thought was that of signs, or pantomimic, next to which, beyond doubt, stands the "Picture Language," which we find carried to perfection in the hieroglyphics of Egypt.

umph, marching into apprehended brotherhood. In all these ages of celestial teaching, Trapper, the future was not hidden from the present nor dead from living. They did come at call and ghostly terrors were not known. The earth-born died; but not as those whose lives have ended, but have just begun. The heavenly ones died not until within immortal veins death entered, as I will tell, by wrong, unfit admixtures of the lower with higher blood. Of this I will now speak.

"Trapper, religions change. They flood and ebb like tides. The old die out and new ones come. They are deciduous. A thousand years, — which in the cycle of existent things are only as are years to centuries, — their leaves, nutritious, medical, fall for the healing of the nations, then they leafless, sapless stand, and are from habit worshipped for other thousand years, though out of them all power for good is gone, and the once vital growth for human need stands, cold and bare, a rigid system of devout formality. The Deity changes also with the changes of the human mind, growing and shrinking as it grows and shrinks in knowledge. Men of different climes and ages give Him different names and nature. Now He is this, now that. According as they know or dream or feel, so is He. Man makes his Deity, and worships the pictured idol of his mind whether false or true, and, worshipping, grows into likeness of his idol whether good or bad.

"But, Trapper, listen and remember what I say; for it is true. Back of all these changes and these picturings of men, good, bad, or both or neither, there stands forever the Eternal Power who made and makes all things by spoken word immediate or slow evolving law, as seemeth to Him good and answereth His own purpose best. The *I Am* of the Jew, the Zeus of Greece, the Jove of Rome, the Sacred Fire of Persia, the Odin of the North, the Manitou of Red Man, the God of Christian is evermore the same; the One Great Deity, the Cause, Creator, Ruler, Preserver of universal man, animals and things. We know He is our Father. That is all we know. The propagating principle strikes its deep root into His own white vitalness, and from it draws unintermittent sap and is forever active. Beyond this simple fact, self-evident, we nothing know. All else is born of fancy, wish or ignorance, or that infernal pride and cruelty of scheming, grasping priestcraft, which manufactures attributes of terror, digging hells and walling heavens in, that it may hold the keys of them and dominate, through fear, the lives of women and the souls of men.

"This world was made by Him, not as a special act, to loom forever, vast and high, in the blue sky of universal sight; nor as a theatre on whose eye-compelling stage great tragedy is played that He might make exhibit of His Love and Power: for He is always making worlds innumerable and filling them with races, as He, in summer, fills meadow-land with flowers. For when He made, He made it as a residence and home for earth-born and for spirits both, who, for ages numberless, uncalendared, had grown in grace and knowledge of finest arts and holy things;

and these to earth came down to give the new earth knowledge and to teach the lowly ones of clay the science of pure life and lay in law and helpful order broad and deep the strong foundations of development, that they in time might grow to their estate and so have freedom of the Universe. Thus was it, Trapper, and no other way, as I and other like me have had from record, memory-kept, handed down to us from that first day when they, the Stars of Morning, sang welcome to the new-made world and songs of praise to Him, the Maker.

"So was it at the first. The earth was free to all, and heavenly ones came down as knowledge comes to ignorance, to teach it and assist. These were the White Ones of the world, the mighty Sons of God, and were, by right of knowledge and of power, the rulers of the earth. They taught it science, gave it laws, transmitted hither arts of building and of healing, tested the qualities of earthly things,— its minerals, ores and precious gems,—divided base from pure, measured the orbit of the earth, its axis calculated and fixed its place among the constellations which rule its motion, and gave them names familiar to the ears of lower earth-born men.[1] These mighty

[1] It is plain that in early ages mankind were divided into Totemic sects or families bearing animal names. From this arose the fables of animals having human speech. When we read in some old author that the Fox talked with the Crow or the Wolf to the Sheep, it simply means that a man of the Fox Totem or Tribe talked with a man of the Crow Tribe, or one of the Wolf family with one who bore the Sheep as his Totem or family name. It would be natural, as Astronomical knowledge grew and stellar discoveries were made, that the forming

ones, these teachers from the skies, these wise and holy beings were the gods of earth, and so they stand to-day in all the ancient literatures,—grotesque, weird, meaningless, because their cause, their order and their old significance are lost and scattered, crudely woven into later superstitions,—mere shreds and patches of a glorious fabric that once was perfect whole.[1]

constellations should receive these Totemic names, in compliment, perhaps, to the Tribes or Nations that bore them. It is as if astronomy were now forming the constellations and grouping the starry systems and should call one the Constellation of England, and another of Russia, instead of Saturn or Orion.

[1] The Mythologies of Greece and Rome are unquestionably based on great facts of personal existences and actual history that belong to remotely early ages. Neptune, Jove, Hercules, Mars, Vulcan, these were all once men, kings, rulers, noted benefactors of the human race

"Now hearken. When first the Sons of God, the gifted ones of Heaven, came visitant to earth, — which was not till the slow evolving movement of creation had, through ages long, circled its full sphere, and earth and all its creatures perfect stood, — they found on earth a race of beings strangely born. They had come upward by evolving[1]

and not mere creations of the fancy of Grecian and Roman poets. They are the shades or ghosts of once living, substantial persons, whose natural forms are lost to the historic eye in the dim distances of unrecorded times and so are therefore seen in grotesque misshapenness.

[1] This old Nasquapee Conjurer or Prophet had evidently a pretty correct conception of Darwin's system or idea of evolution. It might be interesting to inquire whence he derived his knowledge so closely in accordance with advanced modern thought on the development of the human species.

growth and were of many orders. Each bore in mind or mood, in body sturdy or light, a dim resemblance to his or her original. In each, by motion, look, by style of voice or eye, by color, management of form or characteristic passion, was hint of prototypes in distance hidden.

"Some were as tigers, fiercely strong and beautiful with wild and savage beauty, softening into purring moods at times, and sweet maternal tendernesses. Some were lithe and subtle as the snake when, sinuous and glossy with new skin, he charms the innocent bird to his keen fangs. Some had the haughty loneliness of the snow-headed eagle, and his eye to gaze undazzled at the sun, when, soaring high o'er cloud and shade through crystal air with steady wing in level flight, he grazes its hot rim and glances, with shrill scream of challenge, onward; — that scream which hunters trailing on in silence hear come hissing, tearing downward like a burning arrow, and wonder what the awful sound may be and whence it came. Swift and strong to swoop and strike were they, and death flew with their shadow. Nor lacked these earth-born races skill to make and build, for they were cunning with the cunning of the bee and ant and those winged architects which weave their homes from textile hair, from gossamer floss or floating fibres, and hang them pendent by shrewd fastening from the swaying bough. But they were fickle, fierce or ignorantly weak, and had no common language and lacked the mind to organize and push on and up to final finish what they set hand to. So nothing of their doing was carried to perfection, or broadly based to stand the wear of time and shocks of change. Hence all they did fell down in ruin ere 'twas done, and all their progress was in circles moving round and round in endless imperfection.

"But of their women, there were some whose loveliness was hued and odored like the earth, their mother, when amorous warmth sweetens her swelling breasts with bloom and spice; and pungent odors fill the nose with pleasure and with longing for more and deeper inhalations. Dark were these women, but glorious as the night when through its spaces of warm dusk the stars are powdered thick and all its swarth is flushed with latent light and heat. Some were superbly calm,—their movements as the swan's, slow, stately, proud, reposeful as still pools vine-bordered, starred with lilies, — on whose bosoms, warm and sweet, a man might sleep forever nor wish to wake. Blooded were some like fire, veined with passions swarth as hot as torrid heat in jungles, electric as the night when all the gloom sweats odors which o'ercome the senses, and in it, latent, lurks the unkindled lightning. In some were strange magnetic powers, known or unknown to them, and he on whom, when place and time and mood were apt, they slowly fixed their orbed eyes, half-closed, voluptuous, lost higher wit and virtue and every sense save sweet receptiveness, and yielding, overcome, did gently sink into their gracefully lifted arms as into sweetest heaven. Some won by gentleness and goodness, being of mild natures, dispositions sweet, modest and shy as antelopes or the gazelle, and lovely as untutored grace might be and that sweet modesty which, startled at first thoughts of love, shrinks timid from the sight of its own loveliness. These women of the Earth, novel to Heaven's sight, lifted eyes of homage to the Sons of God, wise, strong and holding kingly rank, and in the splendor of their beauty lay at their feet in humble worship, graceful, solicitous, enticing. Nor did they fail in their wild, natural wooing. For they were honest in it, being all enthralled with glorious face and form and spectacle of rank, and, more than all, their loveliness was great. So were the White Ones of the world, pure-blooded, deathless Sons of God, drawn downward to the lower type in amorous admiration, and took of them wives as many as they chose.[1]

"So ruin came to the first world and order. The pure crossed with the impure lost their purity for aye. The mountain streams flowing crystal from the fount of God, fell into valley pools and were forever roiled. The temper of the skies, serene and sweet, was roughened and made sour. The bright intelligence of Heaven, quick to invent, to see, to analyze, fashion and construct, was clouded; the even disposition thrown from its poise, the . just judgment warped, the holy, vital force to will and do, running clear from the Font of Life, grew thick with earthly mixtures. All cer-

[1] Genesis vi. 2.—The Sons of God saw the daughters of men, earth-born, that they were fair. And they took them wives of all which they chose.

tainty of holy birth was lost. The propagating instinct, drawn from God, was turned against Him, for mongrelism,[1] — that worst and deadliest sin, corrupting all, — was lifted on to thrones that ruled the world, and, with power perverted ever after, helped to mar it.

"So fell the race of God. So virtue went forever from the earth, and sin came in. The

[1] The practice of "out crossing" as it is called by breeders was, evidently, not favored by the Divine Parent of the human race as he everywhere set law and custom against it. There is not a race that has ever gained, symmetrically, by marrying beyond its own blood. The pure-blooded, inbred races are those who reached and maintained a high level of excellence. The Jews, Egyptians, Greeks, Romans, Irish, might all be quoted in support of this position. The idea that a great, symmetrically formed race can ever be built up in this Continent on the basis of nationalized mongrelism is scouted by all history. God and history are alike against it.

leaders of the blind were blinded, and both fell down together into deepest ditch. As entered mortal mixtures into deathless veins, death entered, not as new birth from lower unto higher at full-time pregnancy, but as doom, and with each added birth there came new risk and ruin to mankind. Like poisonous vapor out of noxious pools, rising cold and dank, death slowly up the shining slopes of tainted generations rose, until in darkness it enveloped all from basest hut to noblest throne. And thus with sin against pure blood came death into the world.

"Thus the first glory of the world went down in ruin. The tree of knowledge, whose fruit your Scriptures say the woman ate, — a fable growing out of fact, a withered leaf of old-time knowledge, fragrant still, garnered by poet out of Jewish lore, garnered by Jew in turn from literatures that had it full in prose and verse a thousand and ten thousand years before the day that Abraham or even Job drew breath,—was marriage with the Gods, from which,—as was in nature sure to be,—came power to hand and knowledge into heart and head, which they, earth-born, untaught, undisciplined, weak or wicked, knew not how to use aright, or, knowing, because of evil in them, perverted it to evil use. The sin was not on woman, but on him, who, for his wanton pleasure, lifted her to marriage bed beyond her dignity, and to familiar sight of powers and forces, agencies and agents, that were beyond her ken or skill to understand or use aright. She was forbid to taste the fruit of that forbidden tree as childish ignorance, inquisitive, is commanded not to touch the fire that burns. But more was he a hundred times forbid who lifted her unto its branches sweet with flower and odorous leaf, and put the luscious fruit into her longing mouth. The woman erred unconscious, striving to reach and have what to her senses was sweeter than the breath of life to nostril, according to the longing of her ambitious, ardent nature. But the man she tempted, or was tempted by, who did lift her up, from love or lust, unto the level of forbidden bed and all the life and knowledge which, through wifehood, motherhood and daily intercourse, it gave, did sin against the dignity of his high nature and a law which in his clear intelligence blazed warningly as blazes beacon fixed above the rocks of wreck and death.

CHAPTER VI.

THE WHITE GOD OF MISTASSINNI.

"THUS in the beginning gained the earth whatever it has had of glory. It gained. It lost. For of the mingling of the higher with the lower, there came, not all at once but gradually, a lapse and weakening of that vital force which had come down from heaven; a clouding of that bright intelligence which only cycles of eternity can give the seeking mind; a lowering of the tone and level of ambition, which erst sought only noble ends; and, worst of all, a lapse in holiness. The pure imagination was befouled, a grossness came to appetite, the moral sense was blunted

—that sentinel of God, which, while it stood instinct with heavenly life, kept perfect guard above sweet innocence and trustful virtue.

"So passed the ages, and the earth grew upward in external glory but downward into moral ruin. Then shocks were felt which shook the solid world. Catastrophes were multiplied. Here Fire, there Water, and at some other point Frost wrought its work of ruin. Chaos had come again. The Motherland sank under sea, and with it went the treasures and the records of the primeval cycle. Here and there a colony survived and carried down to later ages some feeble fragments of the glorious whole that had been shattered into ruins. Only these survived. The sphered excellence of high achievement, perfect in holiness, glorious as a globe illuminated, proof of what moral rectitude with mortal power might do, was lost forever.

"Then out of space there came a vagrant world flying in unguided, lawless flight; a world on fire, — a funeral pyre of some old race, perhaps — and as it passed, monstrous in size, flying faster by ten thousand times than this small globe wheels on, nigh to that point which now is northern pole, the home of Arctic cold, which then was Summer-land,[1] where dwelt, 'mid flowers that faded not and fruits that ripened for each day of the round year, my race; it struck the earth, and in the twinkling of an eye my race became extinct.

[1] There is no possible way to explain the presence of many forms of tropic life found, by whalers and Arctic explorers, within the Arctic circle, save on the supposition that a sudden and life-destroying change of climate came, in some prehistoric period, to the polar region.

The level axis of the earth was, by the dreadful shock, knocked obliquely up, the round of Nature's order changed, summer and winter rushed into alternate place, and transposed were the zones. Thus, Trapper, died the first two races of the earth. The one sank under water, and the legend of that flood is told in almost every language of the world.[1] The

[1] It is a remarkable fact that in Egyptian literature, historic or legendary, there is not the least hint of or allusion to the Flood. In Plato's "Atlantis" the aged Priest of the Temple at Sais who entertained Solon, Plato's grandfather, while living in exile out of Greece, accounts for this fully. He explained to Solon — I quote from memory — that the reason why Egypt had no special memory of the Flood was because there had been many such local catastrophes on the earth since the beginning, of which their records had knowledge, and that there was no legend about that special one because the facts of it were all fully known to them.

other perished under shock from heaven which crushed them on the instant. As falls the hammer on the anvil so death fell on them. They knew not it was coming till it came. Beneath that blow they and their mighty works were beaten into dust. The gravel of these northern wilds that mark the landscape is granulation of old palaces. We are within the circle of a ruin that buried half the world as you bury bodies under sand.[1]

"Here at Ungava, where fruits and flowers were then, there was a colony of that old race which lived in Summer-land of the North. This fringe of population, not wholly pure in blood but mixed with other races

[1] This certainly explains that mystery of the earth — the great geological puzzle — the Drift. Whence came it, when and how?

which they met as they pushed southward, escaped, and so remained a feeble remnant of that primal stock that once held all the North. Trapper, this is enough. You know the past. I am of it and of that Caste which 'mid the ancient folk held Sacred Keys of knowledge and of power preserved from earliest days, — a knowledge that knows all that has been, and a power that bridges death and brings across it at my call the feet of those who over it, amid the wailing of their friends, did pass to distant realms. One thing alone remains for me to tell. It is a modern happening, and gets significance from what it means to you and her. Listen now, and hear.

"When he who was the sire of the old tongueless chief of Mistassinni was but a boy, he found, one morn at sunrise, on the beach of that great inland sea far westward of the lake where lived his tribe, a boy of his own age. He lay upon the sand as dead. His face was white as snow. His hair was gold. Upon his bosom there was traced strange Totem, unknown to all the tribes. It was a double letter thus: —  — in color red as blood. He had come over sea in boat not built by hands; at least, so seemed it to the tribes that knew no boat save such as their own hands had fashioned. That boy revived. The young chief fed and brought him by his hand unto the council chamber of his tribe, and all the ancients hailed him as fulfilment of a prophecy old as itself, that, 'After many years, out of the West, in boat not made with hands, should come a god white-skinned with yellow hair.' Thus came unto the tribe of Mistassinni that 'White God,' as he is known through all the North. He grew in stature and in grace; was fair to look upon, and wise. He learned their tongue; his own was all unknown to them. He married princess of our Caste. A son was born. That son am I. To him was born a son of other princess, for our Caste weds within its circle and goes not beyond. That son had child. Enough of this; we will go back. For of this 'White God' would I tell, that you may know him. Then would I a solemn question ask.

"In battle he was chief. He was not large in stature, but as the fight roared on and hotter grew he grew in size until at the white heat of it he filled the field. His presence was an atmosphere, which, being breathed, made those who breathed it braver, so that each lifted arm in the long ranks that saw him fight struck downward as if muscled to his shoulder. He flamed the fight as lightning, in mid-ocean, on some tempestuous night, flames the black billows. No fear was in him. Battle to his soul was as wedding hour to ardent lover. Through whirling hatchets, circling axes, brandished spears and arrows driving through the air like hail in winter, he would swoop as through the flying leaves, gust-whirled in autumn, eye fixed and talons set, the forest hawk swoops to his quarry. No man e'er lived on whom he set his blazing eye in battle. In peace his face was sunny. Through his yellow beard his skin showed as a girl's. His eye was as a pool, on whose still surface lilies sleep unstirred by breath of wind. But when it came to blows his face grew gray as steel, his eyes blazed bluish black as winter's sky, when all the warmth is frozen out of wave and star and heaven itself is pitilessly cold. But when the fight was over he would take his wounded foes and bear them to his tent and nurse them as a mother her sick child. Many he healed and with strong bodies they went home, to be his foes again and fight him on some other day.

"Once only was he merciless. It was that year that they of Mistassinni hunted seal on the west coast of wild Ungava, where the ebb and flood of icy tides are twenty times the height of man's full stature. One day a ship drove in whirled onward by a tempest from the north, through froth and foam that whitened her black hull a spear's length deep from stern to stem. Onward she drove before the whistling winds, her sails in tatters streaming in thin strips from spar and mast, until the mighty eddy, spinning round 'twixt a great island and main shore, dashed her, side on and downward, with a crash, as she were eider's egg, upon the beach in front of our encampment. One only of her crew survived the shock, and he, a giant, battle-axe in hand, stood on the sand unharmed. We gathered round him as he stood at guard, our seal spears pointed into sand that he might know we fought no man that had been flung by God's swift-handed mercy out of death.[1]

[1] The superstition of an Indian forbids him to kill one who, apparently, had had a miraculous escape from death. Many white men have escaped their vengeance because of this feeling. Captain Rogers, the noted scout,

"Then came our Leader slowly down the slope to where we stood, our peaceful spears in sand, a smile of welcome on his face and light of gladness shining in his eye. So came he and within the circle of our mercy stood. But as his eye fell, at short distance, on the man, his face turned into ice. Its skin grew gray as steel. His eyes two orbs of fire became. From nighest girdle plucked he battle-axe and on the stranger stalked until he came within arm's reach. Then tore furred vestment from his breast until the dreadful Letter painted on his snow-white skin showed red as blood. So stood he posed. In one clinched

who fell or slid safely down the front of the great cliff on Lake George, which was, because of his perilous feat, named after him, is one of the instances out of many which might be mentioned in this connection.

hand was fragment of torn skins, torn from his heart; the other gripped the battle-axe. Thus in the hollow circle of our mercy stood the two, our God and giant stranger. Then out of sockets bulged the giant's eyes. The coarse skin of his cheeks did pallid grow. His black hair, rising slowly, lifted woollen cap from head. His big knees, bigger than joints of moose, shook under his huge bulk. A fit of trembling seized him. Down fell he on his knees while in his monstrous jaws rattled his teeth, fear-shook. Then out of quavering mouth there came a scream, 'Captain, have mercy!' Speechless still, our Leader, without word or sign, upward swung his axe and on the suppliant's head he brought it down so heavily that through the cloven crown its broad base sank to mangled jowl, and the big bone handle flew in fragments to the striker's hand. Then, turning face upon us white as God's own wrath, he said, 'Throw this damned carcass into torrent swift and eddy deep, that they may whirl and float it where my father's soul beyond the northern straits waits to snatch it toward the mouth of hell and thrust his murderer in.' Trapper, thou art white man without cross, and of his race and speech. In battle thou art bigger, but no braver. Who was this White God of rocky Mistassinni? Who was his father? What the red Totem on his heart; the double Letter red as blood? My power is blinded to this mortal thing. Beyond, I might see better. Can'st thou tell?"

"Ay, ay," replied the Trapper. "Prophet, well I know the race of this White God of Mistassinni, who was his sire, and what the double Letter on his breast did mean. The boy who came, wind-blown from out the sea, leagues west of Mistassinni, in boat not built by mortal hand,—because not built of bark,—and lay at sunrise on the beach all wet and foul with brine and sand, and by the old Chief's grandsire there was found, adopted, worshipped as a god by all the tribes, was son of bravest man that ever trod a deck or chanced the dice with death that he might westward find a pathway for the commerce of the world and bring to knowledge of the Cross of God the distant tribes of men. His name, old Seer, was Henry Hudson,[1] and the

[1] I can but refer the reader to the history of early navigators, of whom Henry Hudson was one of the bravest, for a full account of his sad fate and that of

monogram or Totem — call it as you please, as you be red or white — upon his breast, was the two first letters of his name cunningly blent in one. This boy the old Chief's grandsire found upon the beach, was that sweet son of his, scarce more than child, who bravely by his father's side stood up, when by his crew, in cruel mutiny, the boat was pushed from his stout ship, that it might bear them, drifting, unto awful death. Ay, now I know why he was merciless when on Ungava's beach his father's murderer knelt roaring for mercy. God! what a blow in judgment did he strike, and how it eased

his brave boy, when his mutinous crew forced him into an open boat and sent it adrift in the wild waters which now bear his name. Neither he nor his son was ever seen by white men after.

his soul. Prophet, thou art above the common superstitions of the tribes, and I have told you truth. This fabled God of Mistassinni; this White One of the North the tribes do worship, was Henry Hudson's son, a man of my own race and tongue, whose death has been a mystery for twice a hundred years. Go on and tell me all. This is great news. The world of letters and of men beyond these wastes of rock and leagues of rootless snow and ice will thrill with wonder when it learns from thee, through me, the fate of Hudson and his boy. Whom wedded he? Were children born to him? Are any of his name and blood alive, or is the line extinct? Prophet, I swear that I would trail a trail until my head was white if at the end of it my eyes might look upon the face of one within whose veins there flowed the noble blood of Hudson."

Long sat the Prophet silently revolving in his mind what he had heard. His features lighted as a shuttered window, pane by pane, grows out of darkness, with the coming of the dawn. His eyes of night glowed under brows of snow as to the Trapper's face he lifted them. Then slowly out of parting lips there came the words, "In cheek of snow that thou hast seen, John Norton, runs this mighty blood. Thy head need never whiten on the trail that leads thee to thy wish. The face that thou would'st see, lies there on yonder couch of skins. Ungava is the child of the White God. She ends the line."

Then up the Trapper rose. His face white as Ungava's, as she lay unconscious on the couch of skins whose fur was black as jet digged in the caves of night. A moment stood he dumb. Then said he, standing straight:

"Prophet, thou art a man of many days. Truth should be on thy lips and fear of God. But thou do'st tell a tale so strange that to thy face I say I cannot credit it. Proof there must be of this; proof sure as eye may see. Give me some proof that she, the savior of my life, is of the White God's blood, or I will go my way as one who hears an idle story told."

Then slowly from the chair of polished horns the Seer of many days with stately motion rose. His pale face paler grew, and his thin hand, on which the stone of mystic power blazed red, trembled with passion.

"Never before," he cried, "since from my

sire, as God did take him,[1] received I ring of power and wand that burns because I will it, has mortal doubted word of mine, and lived. Thou art my guest and ignorant, thou mighty man, therefore I do forgive. Linked, also, is her soul with thine, and how or what the issue is to be, for good or ill, I know not. Hence let it pass. Do'st thou ask proof; proof such as eye can see? Come hither then. Fear not; the trance in which she slumbers sweetly holds all senses locked. Behold, from breast of snow beneath which dwells her spirit pure as that white star that never moves from where it sentinels the centre of all worlds and systems which move obedient round it, I lift this virgin vestment. Tell me, thou doubting man, do'st thou see

[1] "And Enoch was not, because God took him."

sign that cannot lie? Is not Ungava child of the White God?" And lo! with starting eyes the Trapper saw, in color red as blood, the double Letter on her bosom white as drifting snow!

"Enough, enough," he cried in solemn tones. "It is enough. That is a sign that cannot lie. Ungava is the child of your White God! By all I hope and long for in the world to come, I would we two had never met!"

CHAPTER VII.

THE COUNCIL OF THE CHIEFS.

THEN came a runner, running from the south. O'er fields of sand ploughed by the winds in ridges; over stretches of blocked ice, cracked into squares, blue, green, and white, — a strange mosaic of gigantic size, — he sped as if some dreadful death was speeding on his trail. From village unto village did he run, and as he ran he cried:

"To arms! to arms! the Esquimaux are coming! A thousand warriors armed for fight, and at their head an ancient chief stalks on."

So ran he and so cried his wild alarm.

Then roared the villages as roars the hollow log when some rude shock has startled hive within. The cry of woman and of child arose. It swelled in vengeful shrillness, strident, fierce as eagle's scream. Out of each warrior's mouth there burst the battle yell, and hatchets edged for death flashed in the air.

Then flocked the chiefs to council, and the Indian Parliament was held, — that place of high debate where nature's eloquence is heard and noble speech leads up to nobler deeds. No idle word is spoken there. No wily politician counsels for self-gain. Each word is from the heart. Each sentence like sure stroke of axe; and they who speak, speak for the good of all, and every statement or appeal is backed with readiness to die.

In the high hall of that old cavern they did meet. The man of ancient days sat in his awful chair, carved into shapes fantastic, weird, hewn from wood unknown among the timber of the world to-day, bristling with polished horns whose every point shone like a star, and standing on the pavement black as night, whose gloom was lighted with the signs of Zodiac in brightest gold. On this strange seat, mysterious, the Wizard sat, Head of the Council. Upon his banded brows were horns of burnished gold. Midway between their roots, large as a star, a diamond blazed. The mystic Rod was in his stronger hand. Upon the other gleamed the dreadful Ring, instinct with conscious fire. Pale was his face. His hair, snow-white as whitened wools, lay on his shoulders thin. Beneath his brows projecting, glowed his eyes, bright with concentrate light.

Thus was he seated. On his right the Trapper sat, strong-featured, grave of face, observant. On his left, the Chief of Mistassinni, withered, bloodless, thin, as body that had risen out of old embalmment. Then inward filed, with slow and stately pace, the chieftains of the Nasquapees. Each in the solemn circle took his place. Each on the earth fixed eye and silent sat. No glance of fire, no moving lip was there. They sat as sit the dead in circle placed. The silence of the chamber might be felt. Thus sat they taciturn and grim, while hour-glass would have run its sands half out.

Then slowly rose an aged chief. His head was gray with years, but straight he was as is the pine's trunk when its crest is shorn. Up rose he straight, and stood. Searched with his eye each tawny face with glance of fire; cast blanket down until the Totem showed above his heart; and on his breast an ochred death's-head grinned; then said:

"Men of Ungava, Nasquapees, straight standing men,[1] the hated Esquimaux are

[1] If you ask a Montagnais Indian what Nasquapee means, he will tell you an atheist, or one who has no God, because the Nasquapees have no medicine-map. But if you ask a Nasquapee what his tribal name means, he will tell you "a man who stands straight." He will tell you, moreover, that he believes in two Great Spirits, a God and Evil One, and that the reason his tribe never had a medicine-man is because they have a great Prophet who is of the old race whence they all sprang, and that he knows all things and can call the dead back to life when he wishes.

coming! I smell them in the air.[1] They stink like rotting seal. Their bodies lie unburied like fish upon the banks of Peribonka, after freshet. They come to die. The blood of other days is in our veins. We of the Ancient Folk know how to fight. My knife is thirsty. It knows where to drink. Look at my axe. See, it is dull with rust. I'll brighten it to-morrow on their skulls. Whose are these arrows? Look! Are they not clean as are the arrows of a boy? It is so long since their steel heads were driven into flesh. I am a boy myself! When have I seen a foe? It is not gray of years upon

[1] As I have said in a previous note, the Nasquapees are noted for the delicateness of their scenting faculty, being as a dog is in this respect. Their sense of smell is simply marvellous.

my head. Some other boy in playfulness has sprinkled ashes there! We Nasquapees have been asleep. Awake. Remember. Look at my breast. That hole will hold a fist. An Esquimau stabbed me there. It was that day we fought them on the Marguerite. See where his seal spear pierced. It drove clean through. Look at my back. Beneath the shoulder blade the head came out. To-morrow in the ranks of death I'll find the dog that drove it in, and pay him the old debt."

And, gathering up his blanket over bosom scarred with dreadful wound, he sat him down, while round the lowering circle vengeful murmurs ran.

Then up stood other one. The horns of power were on his head. Around his neck a string of polar claws gleamed white. One eye was gone. The other blazed like coal of fire blown hot. The glowing orb he fixed in turn on each swarth face in silence. Then stretched to fullest length his sinewy arm, and spake:

"Warriors of the North! Sons of sires that lived in the beginning, what foe has ever seen your backs in battle? Your blood a hundred times has reddened ice on cold Ungava, and fell in battle rain on its coarse gravel. We are a thousand knives. One for each knife comes on. Upon that field above the sounding sea where for a thousand years our sires did fight, there will we fight to-morrow. Look at my face. Where is my other eye? Whose spear's point bored it out? Look at my breast. You cannot see it. It is hidden under scars. Who made them? White Wolf, where is your oldest son? His bones are bleaching on the sands of Mamelons. I saw him fall beneath the axe of Esquimau. His spirit wanders unavenged. Black Bear, where are your children? The Esquimau dogs on the flat banks of Peribonka ate them. Gray Fox, where is your youngest daughter? She toils a slave, beaten by Esquimau whips, at Labrador. Is the old blood frozen in us? No. It burns like fire in autumn rushes. The dead are looking at us. They are bursting out of graves to see if we be men. Listen. Hear. Their voices call for vengeance. One day, give us one day of glorious battle, and we will feed the hungry wolves of wild Ungava fat with flesh of Esquimaux."

So thundered he, and at the closing word

of the maimed warrior, up with a yell the circle leapt, and twenty axes lifted high flashed gleaming brightly through the cavern's gloom.

Then on the left of the great chair the Chief of Mistassinni rose, tongueless, withered, thin with age, but his old frame, charged with electric hate, quivered with life intense, while in his head his eyes glowed like a panther's, crouching for his spring. Then every horny point bristling round the Wizard's seat burned brighter, kindling with fiercer fires; and as the cavern filled with whitest light, around the swarthy circle ran an awful murmur:

"*The dead have risen! Old Mistassinni from his grave above the Saguenay, coming out of dead-land, stands in our council!*"

Then murmur died in silence, while in the

white light stood the old-time chief, and signed:

"Men who stand straight. Sons of the ancient race who once ruled half the world, I, tongueless, speak to you in that old language which has come to you from the beginning. I am a chief of other days. Your fathers knew me. I was their friend, and in their aid have fought upon the sands of wild Ungava here, while you were yet unborn. You know my fame, for it filled all the north. Above the Saguenay I stood the test.[1] I was at torture stake. An Esquimau tore my tongue from out my mouth, and ate it. Then lighted he the fagots. I did not die. Behold, he who sits there — a man without a cross,

[1] An expression used by an Indian to state that he has stood the torture of the torture stake.

white as your God, but red as bravest chief at heart—did rescue me. I lived, and ever since have waited for my day and chance. To-morrow I will fight with you. Your Prophet, he who seeth all in living-land or dead-land, has said that with the Esquimaux my foe is coming. It is well. In battle shall I die, and leaving dead upon the sands my hated foe, I, joyful, will take trail which leads me to my sires. Sons of those with whom in other days I fought; men who stand straight; children of that old race that once ruled half the world; I, of Mistassinni, will fight the Esquimaux with you to-morrow. I have said."

So spake the tongueless chief in stately language of old days, the vivid speech of pantomime,—that quick and universal tongue of ancient races; and as he sat, the warrior circle rose and facing toward the aged man who had been friend and ally of their sires ere they were born, each warrior, hand on breast, bowed low in stately courtesy to the ground.

Then, after pause, the Trapper rose; and every eye in the dark circle fixed itself in admiration on his mighty frame.

"Men of the North," he said, "your fame is known to me. My name, perhaps, is known to you. I am the friend of yonder aged chief, and was the friend of him whose bosom bore the Tortoise sign, who stemmed the bloody tide with you at Mamelons in that dread fight which God by darkness stopped.[1] I am John Norton."

[1] Referring to the dreadful fight at the mouth of the Saguenay, which the earthquake finally stopped. (See the Doom of Mamelons.)

Then out of every mouth there burst a cry of wonder and applause. Each swarthy hand dashed upward, palm outward, unto him, and every feathered head bowed to the cavern's floor. Then spake he farther:

"I have come northward with the Chief to see him fight last fight, and prove my love for him by doing as he bids. No greater proof has love than that to give. To-morrow he will find among the Esquimaux his foe. You are the sons of sires who never, beaten, left a bloody field, and need no help from me. I will stand by and see the old Chief has fair fight. So has he bidden and so will I do. I am his friend, and with him keep I word and bond. I have said." And, as he closed, a murmur of assent ran round the circle dark.

Then from his chair the Wizard spake, and as he spake the lights burned fading down, and at the closing word the chamber filled with gloom:

"My children, I, your Prophet, High Priest of that old race which once ruled half the world, of which you are, Ancient of Days, speak words of Fate. To-morrow you shall fight and win. The Chief of Mistassinni shall find foe and chance. In dying he shall put the Trapper under word and bond, and you shall see such fight as never yet was seen on wild Ungava, where fights have been for twice a thousand years. Northward the Esquimaux shall never march again. My hour has almost come. Soon shall I rise, as all my line have risen after many years, into the skies, not knowing death. None of our Caste has ever entered grave. God takes us.[1] Ungava will go westward to that lake to which of old the White God came. You shall not see her ever more. The race that was with ours in the beginning has died, and ours is dying. Fate has it so, and who may alter fate! But make the sunset of my going glorious. To-morrow fight as you nor any ever fought before, that I may feel the pride of ancient days and bear with me a glorious message to your sires as I join them in the skies beyond the northern fires. I, Seer and Prophet, Ancient of Days, have spoken. Go."

And, as he ceased, the lights died out, and through the gloom was heard the sound of softly going feet.

. . . . .

[1] Genesis v. 24.—And Enoch was not, because God took him.

Next day beheld the lines of battle set. A thousand on each side, they stretched across the plain on which a hundred fights had been in other days. On graves where slept their sires, the living stood, ready to die. Then joined the battle. The hostile lines in charging columns met, and out of war's red mouth an awful bellowing poured. Amid the Nasquapees, upon the left, the tongueless Chief of Mistassinni fought. Gray, withered, dumb, he seemed a warrior out of dead-land. He spake no word; from mouth no yell of triumph came, nor order; but silently he killed. The Esquimaux before the dreadful apparition fled. They cried: "The dead have risen! who can the dead withstand!" and ran.

Upon the right, heading the Esquimaux, another ancient warrior, gray, withered, dumb, fought in same dreadful style. The Nasquapees, affrighted at the awful sight, fled crying: "The dead have risen! This is no living warrior;—who can the dead withstand!" Thus either end of battle line bent backward and gave way before the ghostly sight.

Then to the Chief of Mistassinni a wounded warrior ran, and cried: "On the far right a warrior risen out of grave is driving all before him. Come and help." And to the Esquimaux there came a runner, running as for life, and said: "Come to the other end of battle, for out of death has come a chief of ancient days who driveth all before him." And thus the two old chiefs, who long had waited for this day of vengeance, came hurrying toward each other, and, midway between the scattered wings, met face to face, at last!

So did the two old apparitions stand mid-way betwixt the lines, grim, silent, glaring at each other, gathering strength for battle unto death. And all the war grew silent as the two, and stood at rest, waiting to see the awful fight begin.

CHAPTER VIII.

DUEL OF THE OLD DUMB CHIEFS.

THEN each his hatchet threw, and all the might of their old withered arms went with the deadly cast. The bright blades whirling on met in mid flight, and steel and handles shivered at the shock like glass. Then up from either line of faces battle-painted, ochred in panoply of death, rose a shrill yell as the war hatchets shivered, — a sight no warrior standing there had ever seen before, though some were gray in war and scarred with half a hundred battles. But on the heel of that wild yell of thoughtless rage and pride, the prophets of each tribe sent forth a wail, low, wild, and long as is the cry of crouching, shivering hound above the dying hunter, — dying in the snow. For well they read the sign, and knew that never yet had warriors lived whose axes met midway between their heads and shivered in the air.

Then the two aged, tongueless foes drew bow and loosened quiver, and quick as lightning's flash set shaft to tightened string. The air between them on the instant thickened with flying shafts; the rounded shields of walrus hide, hung from their necks above each shrivelled breast, rang like two anvils tapped by falling hammers as the steel-headed arrows smote them. So rained and rang the bolts of death upon the two opposing shields, and, when the sheafs were spent, their tawny, shrunken arms and shoulders were cut and pierced with gashes red and deep, and blood fell downward from their wounds as fall the first drops from a cloud before the thunder rolls; while at their feet the feathers from the broken shafts lay thick as plumage in a glade above whose turf two hungry, hunting eagles, swooping at one prey, have met in mad and disappointed swoop, and clinched. But by no bolt had either shield been pierced, and underneath the tough, protecting hides their old mad hearts, untouched, beat, hating, on.

Then rose a mighty murmur, and each line of battle, forgetful of its hate, swayed in around the fighters; for never on wild Ungava's stormy shore, where bloody war had been for twice a thousand years, had there been seen by mortal eyes such dreadful fight before. It was as if these two old chiefs had burst their cerements of bark and risen out of graves, shrivelled, dried, death-dumb, to *fight*, and show the younger men that gazed, how their old grandsires fought it out. The Trapper, leaning on his rifle not ten paces off, saw in the gloomy orbs of the old Chief the death light shine, and knew that this was his last battle. Thrice lifted he his rifle butt from sand, then drove it back. Thrice did his mighty fingers seek hatchet handle, then fall away, and with a groan he said:

"Nay. Nay. It may not be. It is a mighty fight and fair. My God! it must go on! But his old eyes will never gaze again on the loved rocks of Mistassinni!"

Thus mingled were both wars. The Esquimau stood side by side with hated Nasquapee. Their painted faces almost touched as they stood thronged around the dreadful two whose hearts were hot with hate kindled in old fights fought on those barren shores before the warriors round them had been born.

Then the two fighters, grim and gray, with stately motion lifted their old hands, palm outward, and called mutual truce. Then signalled the gray Esquimau in dumb show to his tribe:

"My children, here fight I my last fight. My fathers call me, and I go. The trail has waited long and I must tread it now. This chief and I have met before. With this right hand I tore his tongue from out his mouth. Lying half smothered in the brands, his hand launched knife at me, which passing through my face made my mouth dumb forever. We both have wrongs to right, and we will right them here. Take ye my body to that bold bluff where all my fathers sleep abreast of Anticosti. Lay me with them there where I may hear the tides come roaring in, and see the seals at play. Let there be wail for me as for an old-time chief among the tents which empty stand and will stand empty ever more beside the sea whose moan shall sound forever for a race forever gone. From this last field of mine bring into Spirit-Land such news of deeds and death as shall make welcome for you such as warriors give and get around those spirit fires which light the lodges of our sires beyond the northern sky. I, dying, give cheer to you about to die. So fare you well."

Then to the Trapper signalled his dumb friend:

"Trapper, the trail is ready and I go. This Esquimau and I will end our quarrel here. The trail is long and lonely, but never yet hast thou failed dying man. I love thee, Trapper, for thou art true. No white is in thee. Thou art red. I shall not see thee ever after this. Thy trail runs to the front of Atla's throne; mine to my father's lodge. Tell her from me, that he who made her grave at Mamelons sent greeting to her when he died. Take thou my body to far Mistassinni and lay it in that cave where sleep my sires and where forever sound the voices of the dead. When we have ended this, let these damned Esquimaux feel thy rifle butt and knife. At sunset, out of this last fray of mine, let both come forth well wet with brains and blood. It is my last behest. I love thee, Trapper, like a chief. So give me word and bond. May no knife ever girdle head of thine. So fare thee well."

Then spake the Trapper:

"Old friend, as thou hast said, so shall it be, if life holds with me after this. Thy greeting will I give her when we meet. Thy body will I bear to Mistassinni, and, in the cave where sleep thy sires and where their voices sound forever, there shall it sleep. These dogs of Esquimaux shall feel my rifle butt and knife. From this last fray of thine they shall come forth both red and wet. I give thee word and bond. So lay on, Chief, and make thy vengeance sure. Thy heaven may not be mine; and so I say my long farewell, and give thee dying cheer."

Then once again the old gray haters faced, and their throats rattled, struggling with wild yells. Their sunken eyes glowed hot as burning coals. They dashed their shields to earth and stooped low down. Then drew their knives, long, bright, and keenly edged; sprang into air and met, — and *struck*. Each knife drove, heart-deep, home; and, as they fell apart, each bosom held the other's blade sunk 'twixt the ribs to the strong handle. So they died.

Then for a space was silence. Deep as death's, it hung above the host and stayed the pulses of the air. Then into it and through it, swelling slowly up and wavering on, the Indian wail arose, wild and weird, the saddest of all wailing ever sounded out of throat of woe. Quavering it swelled, lingered in long plaint, then died away in thinnest sound, and all the bloody plain was silent as the grave again. Then, suddenly, like crash of thunder in the breathless pause of some hot summer night, there burst a yell that ripped the silence into fragments. It burst from out a thousand throats as if the thousand had been joined in one, and through it hell had sent from out her caves its scream of hottest hate. Then deadly strife went down and rioted among them. Mixed and jammed they were together. Each man found foe beside him. No room for arrow or for spear was there. Each hand set fingers into nearest throat until their nails in torn flesh met. Then knives were plucked and reddened to the handles as they found flesh, and half the battle in the sand lay coiled and knotted like a field of snakes. So wrestled they and clung, bit, struck, and died.

When rose the signal yell the Trapper's rifle cracked. Both barrels rang almost in twin report and two tall chiefs sank brainless to the sand. Then, swinging heavy hatchet in mighty hand, into the jammed battle did he, headlong, plunge. Half through the thickened throng of fighting men he hewed his way. Through lifted shield his red axe sank to covered head and clove to shattered jaw. The warding spear shaft, gnarled and thick, shivered like rod of glass beneath his dreadful stroke. He warded neither knife nor spear. The terror of his arm was his defence. In his red wake the Nasquapees rushed in. They guarded safe and sure the back of their great friend. He knew it not. He only saw his thickening foes in front, and strode straight on. He grew in rage as grew the fight. In him war stood incarnate, fierce and red. The ancient dead fought in him. For o'er his head he heard the steady tramp of feet, and through the air the old Iberian murmurs run. And 'mid the whiz of arrows, whir of hatchets, crash of axes, and the thug of spears as they were driven home, he heard a voice he knew cry clear and loud:

"Lay on, John Norton, lay thou on! For the old Tortoise's sake, — whose son thou art, and king shalt be, — show thy full strength this day and make good her right to name thee lord and master to the mighty warriors of her race, now gazing at thee, under lifted shields above Ungava. Lay on, I say, for tribal sign and her!"

Then he went wild. He cast his dreadful axe in air, and, clutching rifle by the muzzle, drove headlong at them. His mighty face, lean-featured, rigid, battle-white, sharp-set as flint edged for the pan, was horrible to see. His great, gray eyes, beneath his shaggy brows, were black as night, in whose black centre lightnings burn and blaze.

From left to right — a mighty sweep — his heavy rifle swept. Stock, locks, and wood-work shivered as he struck, and flew in splinters wide cast. Around him centred all the battle. He was the battle. Ahead of him the Esquimaux rallied thick as bees in bush, when some intruding shock has burst the hive, and inner comb and dome of gray lie on the ground in patches. Through buckskin shirt and jacket stout their pelting arrows stung. They spotted him with blood. He felt no smart nor sting, but like a maddened lion ramped on. In Esquimaux no coward blood e'er flowed. They are a hardy stock, and all their lives are lived in peril. They breasted bravely up against him by the score, their coarse hair bristling and their small eyes adder-red. On shoulders broad and stout, on thickened skull and wide breast-bone, the bevelled barrels fell and crushed. He smote them down as thresher's flail beats banded bundles on threshing-floor. With every stroke his breathing sounded wide. So fought he, and so they, quivering, died.

Then into the wild battle ran a figure clothed in black. At waist a tasselled cord was tied. His head was shaven bare. In high uplifted hand a silver crucifix gleamed white. Upon a pile of dead men, tumbled like jammed logs, — a dreadful heap of death, — the holy friar leaped and held high the sign of Calvary. Then Nasquapees and Esquimaux dropped on their knees and flung their weapons down. They knelt to Heaven's sign. With steady hand the holy man held silver cross on high, and to the dreadful slayer called:

"Stay hand! Stay hand, thou dreadful man! For Holy Mary's sake and her dear Son's, stay now thy bloody hand! Above this awful field I lift this sacred sign and bid this strife to cease. Let these poor men that live, go free."

Then stood the Trapper. From dripping

brow the battle sweat he wiped with one red hand, and, gripping hard the bloody and bent barrels in the other, said:

"In yonder dell the tongueless Chief of Mistassinni lieth dead. Between his ribs the driven knife still clings. In fair and mighty battle did he die. I was his friend. He knew his doom and bade me long farewell. He loved me like a chief, and therefore charged me, under word and bond, that I come forth from this last fray of his with rifle butt and knife well wet and red with brains and blood. I gave him word and bond, and joyfully he took the trail that led him to his sires.

"Bond and word have I kept on this full field. Above the dead and dying thou hast lifted sacred sign. I am a Christian man.

Let, therefore, these damned dogs go hence alive. They owe me rifle, — barrels, stock and locks, and hatchet flung high up, when in the air I heard her old-time people's war cries ring, and caught the sound of charging feet above my head. I will collect my debt upon them on some other day. Aye, let the dogs go hence. I am a Christian man."

So spake he. Then turned his back on priest and living foe, and, lining steps by the long row of bodies he had smitten down through bloody lane made by his awful rage, he came to where the silent Chief of Mistassinni lay silent evermore.

But when he came to where the old Chief lay, he started, for lo! amid the dead, robed in black furs from head to foot, a hood of night's jet blackness on her head, her serpent wand of twisted gold in hand, her face white as the snow, her great orbs fixed in mournful gloom upon the dead man's face, his withered hand in hers, there sat *Ungava!*

Then spake he, as he stood all dripping red, the wrath of battle in his blood and half its fierceness blazing in his eye.

"Never on battle plain did I see dead so thick! I would that his old eyes had seen a man without a cross keep word and bond. This was last fray of his, and had he lived to see it foughten out, he would have had a tale to tell the chiefs he met as he burst into Spirit-Land that would have sent their hatchets whirling high in air as they gave warrior's welcome. Thou hast seen either world, but did'st thou ever see such fight before, in living-land or dead-land, Ungava?"

Then she made answer. Sitting by the dead amid the dead, and lifting eyes of gloom to his great face, she said:

"Fights many have I seen on sand and ice beneath a sun that neither set nor rose, and under lights no mortal hand e'er kindled in the North, which burned the unseen, rounded end of the world,—but never such a fight as this. Above you, as you onward hewed your way, the old-time dead stood thick as sedge at edge of salted streams in summer. Some were of my red race, for they waved hatchets over head, and on their naked bosoms, crimsoned bright, I saw the Tortoise sign. I knew the Totem, for often have I seen it on the breast of him, your friend, who saved the fight on the flat banks of Peribonka, where my father died. But others did I see, more vast of limb and huge; a giant throng, tall, big-breasted, lofty as pines, who, under oval shields bright as the sun, pure gold, their edges lifted high, gazed at you as you hewed on. And when, at last, thou did'st cast hatchet high in air, and, bare-headed, without guard, did'st beat them down with heavy rifle clubbed, and all its stock and polished woodwork into splinters flew, their mighty swords on golden shields did clash and such a roar went up as never lifted air of either world before. O dreadful man, it was a dreadful fight, and long and wild will rise the wail from maid and wife in the skin tents of Labrador, when from the North there shall be bruited down from tribe to tribe the tidings of this fray on far Ungava. God grant thee mercy, Trapper, when in hour of need he reckons with thee for this dreadful day."

"So be it," gravely answered he, "God grant me mercy full and sure for sin done here or anywhere, when in my hour of need he reckons with me for this fray or other red ones I have fought in. Thou art a girl, Ungava, and can'st not understand a warrior's soul in battle. I did give word and bond to this old chief, my friend, who for the length of warrior's life had walked the vocal world of God with silent mouth, shut off from all he loved and lived for by the great wrong done to him at the stake by the damned Esquimaux. Through savage circle, as they tortured, did I break when blazed the fire they lighted round him. This foot it was that cast the fagots wide, when, from the thongs cut by my knife, he fell headlong among them. For thirty years he lived seeking this day, his foe and chance. Foe and chance did he find on this far field, and mighty battle did he make, though age had whitened head and shrivelled hand. Here, dying, did he put me under bond to right the wrong which he had borne for half a life. So stood the matter. I fought for friendship and for right, and God will grant me mercy, if, in battle fiercely set, I did in wrath strike one red blow too heavy or too many. So let it rest until I come to where the scales are poised for warriors and for wrongs righted in battle. I will bide issue like a Christian man, not doubting. Now will I lift this withered frame that once held mighty soul, and bear it to the cave where you shall fit it for long journey toward the grave which waits its coming at Mistassinni. For there, in that dread cave where all his fathers sleep and where he will sleep the last of all thus chambered, must this old frame be laid: that cave whose fame fills all the North, whose caverned passages, as you know, are filled forever with the voices and the murmurs of the dead.

"So now, old friend, on back of him who keepeth word and bond, from thy last field and fray thou shalt be borne. A heavier burden I have often carried, but never sadder. Ah me! ah me! the dead grow fast and friends grow few as life's swift days fly on! The Queen died on my breast. The Chief is dead. At Mamelons my sweet love sleeps. And now full half a thousand miles I go with him who made her grave, to his own grave at Mistassinni. Ungava, white of face but dark of soul, die not, lest out of that old cave in the Great Rock I shall come forth into an empty world."

Then tenderly the empty frame which once held mighty soul he lifted on his shoulders broad, and, casting one long look across the field whose fame would be his own till all the tribes died out, he went up toward the Conjurer's cave which stood on the high cliff at whose worn base the great tides rush and roar. Him toiling on, Ungava followed, white of face but dark of soul, whose birth was out of mystery and under doom; whose magic was the wonder of the North; whose voice the dead obeyed; whose touch might heal or kill; whose serpent wand of gold was like that rod that Aaron cast at Egypt's feet; and with her in the cave he left the dead, that she, with strange preserving force, might make it fit for distant journey to its distant grave.

CHAPTER IX.

THE FAIRIES' FAREWELL TO UNGAVA.

"TRAPPER, behold the whiteness of the world. How still it lies, like angel sleeping on a couch of down plucked from the white swan's breast. See how the moon wheels up her rounded orb from out the eastern sea, which whitens at her touch to her own beauty. The waves roll pearly pale and fling their spray in silvery showers far up the gleaming cliffs. The snow is whiter as her beams fall on it, and yonder icy islands shine like mirrors as they meet her face turned full upon them. All things are seen in distance, softly dim as some loved face that gazes at us in our dreams, through the gauze curtains which hang but for an hour between us, dreaming, and the spirit world; soon to be softly drawn aside for our own entrance within that peaceful realm where wait the angels, once our friends. Hark! to the low, soft note of mother-seals calling with sweet interrogation to their babes, safely sleeping in the crystal crevices of the ice. Was ever scene more peaceful?"

"It is, indeed, a peaceful scene, Ungava," replied the Trapper, "but barren to the eye of one who loves the stir of life, the motion of the world's activity, the busy hum of going and of coming, and the glow of human happiness. If one could people this pale realm with buoyant motion; set this still air to music and make the moonlight dance, then might he say in truth it were a perfect world produced by magic."

"O, thou of blinded eyes!" Ungava cried. "I did forget thou could'st not see, save as the orbed sentinels on guard beneath the arches of thy beetling brows imperfectly report to thee. What, then, if I should give thee sight which brings the unseen world within my vision, and thou should'st see the Fairies, Sprites, and Elves, the Gnomes and Witches, which people all this winter world, above, around, and underneath us, with frolic and with pleasure, as they hold nightly festival. Would such a sight please thee?"

"Thou art in joking mood," returned the Trapper, smiling. "There are no Fairies in the world; that is the faith of children."

"Children are wiser than the older folk,

John Norton," returned Ungava, seriously. "They come as spirits out of spirit-land, and, taking forms of flesh, are subject to its limitations. O Trapper, this earthly form in which we live, is but imprisonment; bondage to eyes which otherwise might see, and mask to our real faces. Through flesh we only show ourselves in glimpses. And the fond faith of children in the marvellous, to which they cling, is but the struggling of their souls against forgetfulness of that bright, animated world from which they came. And those who laugh at them, because of their sweet credence, are like those blinded ones — the Gnomes of under-earth — who, born in blindness, beyond the reach of light, laugh at our stories of the sun, and smile at us who do put faith in stars. Would'st thou have eyes for once, O Trapper, and see what thou do'st laugh at?"

"My eyes are fairly good," replied he, laughingly. "But if thou can'st give better to me, then, let them come, Ungava."

"Nay, nay, thou sceptic," answered she, "I may not give thee eyes to see what is beyond thy ken at present; but I can command the spirits of the earth and air to take such form as shall upon the lenses of thine eyes cast full reflection, and so become objective to thy senses. They are compliant to me. Shall I call?"

"Aye, call, Ungava, call. If childhood's faith in spirits by any chance be real, I would be child again," he answered, smiling.

Then, as she stood, Ungava lifted wand, and suddenly around the two there grew a light far whiter than the moon. It came as dawn and day would come which had no flush of color. So came it round them as they stood upon the cliff above the lighted sea which darkened with the contrast. So standing in the whiteness, Ungava called:

"Come, Spirit and Sprite,
  Come laughing and dancing;
Come out of the night,
  To this white light come glancing.
Come, Elfin and Fairy;
  I form ring of magic;
Come sing us some song,
  Come dance us some dances.

"Come from sea and from land,
  From deep earth and high heaven,
See, I lift now my hand,
  The signal is given.

From the fires of the North,
  From the foam of the sea,
From your caves now come forth
  And appear unto me!"

Then, slowly, from a mound of snow that lifted dome of whiteness near to where they stood, a form of beauty did arise, clothed in soft vestments woven from whitest fleece and edged with fur of ermine. So into sight she rose, and with her other ones of equal beauty came and, standing in the brilliance, sang:

I.

"I am Queen of the Snow, of the pure white
    snow.
 I eddy and circle and whirl as I go.
 I am Child of the Frost. I am born above
    mountains;
 I mantle the forest; I cover the fountains.

I waver and fall, I stream and I flow,
With the currents of wind. I am beautiful snow!

CHORUS.

"She is Queen of the Snow, of the pure white snow.
We flakes are her subjects: we whirl as we go;
We eddy and circle; we stream and we flow.
She is Child of the Frost. She is beautiful snow!

II.

"When flowers are all withered, and their fragrance is fled;
When the wild grape is fallen, and the green leaf is dead;
When out of the forest the song-birds are flown,
And the harvest is reaped from the seed that was sown;

Then, then, from the sky to the earth far below
I come down in mercy. I am beautiful snow.

CHORUS.

"When flowers are all withered, and their fragrance is fled;
When the wild grape is fallen, and the green leaf is dead;
Then, then, from the sky to the earth far below
She comes down in mercy. She is beautiful snow!"

So sang the elfin ones and vanished, and the white silence softly lay unoccupied on cliff and sea and shingled shore.

"Call yet again," the Trapper cried. "Call yet again, Ungava; for never yet did mortal eyes see sight so sweet, or mortal ears hear sweeter song."

Then lifted she her wand once more, and waved it to and fro as one who beckoning calls. And as the wand in easy circles moved, she, smiling, sang:

"Come, lily so white,
Come out of the night.
Come, rose-tree so red,
Bring wreath for my head.
Let the odor of hill,
 Let the flower of the street,
Let the Spirits of bloom
 Gather here to my feet."

Then, even as she sang, out of the earth there slowly rose a soft green lobe of monstrous size, and opening, lo! The Spirit of the Lilies, in its yellow heart stood forth revealed, — then sang:

I.

"Have you breathed me by night, when on the still air
Came the song of the lute, came the murmur of prayer?
Have you breathed me at morn, when the odorous trees
Were thrilled from their sleep by the kiss of the breeze?
Have you breathed me when mingled with mine was the breath
Of the woman you loved, and must love till death,
As her lips clung to yours, their caress to bestow,
While I lifted and sank on her bosom of snow?
If you have, then you know that no other such bloom
Blows for man or for woman 'twixt cradle and tomb.

II.

"Oh, for love and for lovers my perfume is shed.
I am flower of the living, I am flower of the dead.
At the feasts of the rich, by the lovely and fair,
I am grouped in the cups, I am twined in the hair.
By the hand of the groom, ere he sleeps by her side,
My white leaves are sown on the couch of the bride.
And if she be taken, on the door of her tomb,
As a sign and a symbol, he chisels my bloom.
Oh, for love and for lovers, not since the sweet air
Has been breathed with their sighs has there been flower so fair.

III.

"I am old as the world. When the Stars of the morn
Sang together for joy, for their joy I was born.
In the dawn of the world, when women were given
In their sweetness to men, I was dropped down from heaven,
To be charm for their charms, and a potion, for never
Did a lover love once, and not love forever,
The woman that wore me on her bosom the night
When he knelt at her feet in love's wild delight.
Oh, for love and for lovers, not since the sweet air
Has been breathed with their sighs has there been flower so fair.

IV.

"When the Sons of God chose from the daughters of men
The sweetest and fairest to be wives to them, then
Thy race did begin. When thy first mother was wed,
The stars were made floral to be wreath for her head.
Since then I have come, both for bridal and bier,
When wand has been lifted, or song sung to appear.
Ungava, Ungava, am I needed as breath
In the sweetness of life, or the faintness of death?
Oh, tell me, for ne'er since thy race breathed the air
For love and for lovers has there been flower so fair."

Then silence; and in it lingered long the dying strain, sinking as sinks at death, perhaps, our memory of other days, which we in dying leave regretfully, so sweet they were to us in living, filled to the brim like jocund cup with wit and laughter and love's sweet wine. Then, strangest sight that magic ever gave to wondering mortals, — around the two, on that high cliff, there spread a lawn of emerald, dewy and fresh, in which were floral mounds and clumps of roses whose wealth of bloom weighed the strong bushes down; and hedges fenced it in whose every twig was odorous, and every bush and bloom and leaf was vital. For from this forest sweet a group of fairy, elfin forms, each garlanded with her own flower, came gliding forth and made obedience to Ungava. Then, standing round her, sang:

I.

"Queen of our hearts, by stream and hill,
We heard thy magic summons thrill.
Queen of our hearts, in bower and hall,
We caught the sweetness of thy call.
From Southern pool and stream afar,
We, guided by the Northern Star,
Have come our homage here to give,—
For thee we live! For thee we live!

II.

"Last of that race, whose bridal morn
Was ushered in when we were born;
Last of that race to which we gave,
To sweeten bridal bed and grave,
Our sweetest breath, our fullest bloom;
And laid on cradle and on tomb,
The richest offering we could wreathe,—
For thee we breathe! For thee we breathe!

III.

"Last of thy race! thy eyes of night
Hold in their depths the farther sight.
We are of earth, and may not know
The feeling in thy breast of snow.
We wait thy will. We do not dare
To crown thy head, to wreath thy hair,
Nor garland waist with bridal zone.
Still do we live for thee alone.

IV.

"Last of thy race! perchance 'twill be,
That we thy face no more shall see.
At Mamelons, on breast of snow,
A snow-white lily lieth low;
There on that dreadful hill of fate
Sweet Atla saw her morning break;
But know, in life or death, that we
Still breathe for thee! Still breathe for thee!"

Then died the tender strain, and singers faded with the song, and once again the white silence softly lay unoccupied on cliff and sea and shingled shore. Then she, as waking out of trance, raised eyes of tender gloom to his and said:

"Trapper, behold the sky! What eye may count the stars which to the thoughtful soul do punctuate its spaces with interrogations? Can'st thou believe that all those shining points which powder it with golden dust are worlds, inhabited like ours? See how the o'erarching dome is all bespangled with fretted fire. What noble roofment has this little earth thus canopied with glory! Tell me hast thou a star in yonder sky which thou do'st call thy own? A star linked with a loved one's face?"

"Nay, nay, I am not fanciful, Ungava. I am a plain, blunt man. I know my friends. My foes know me. My loves are simple. I am a man of fact, not fancy. I eat my food. I quench my thirst. I love my friend. I hate my foe. Word and bond keep I unto death. The rest I leave to God."

"But, Trapper, lift thou thine eyes again. Select some star, distant or nigh, and to it link a name — the name of her thou lovest over all. Let its bright ray be to thine eyes a face, and tell me of her. I would know the woman thou do'st love."

"The woman I do love, Ungava, lives not in any star. She lives — I know not where. I know not where to find her when I die. I only know she loves me with a queenly love; and when my eye grows dim and all the trail fades out, I trust her faithful hand will guide me on. I know no further, and I have no further hope."

"But, Trapper, if thy love is dead and gone — forever gone — and where she is thou knowest not, nor how to find her, nor whether you and she shall ever meet. If all is dim, uncertain, dubious, — then thou can'st surely love some other one — some fair, sweet one, who should give all her soul to thee; be comfort to thy days, and to thy face lift eyes of worship because to her thou art as God."

Then said the Trapper, gravely:

"Ungava, of little loves man may have many, born of his vagrant moods or transient passions; for man is as the earth, and out of him, prolific, spring many growths, some sweet, some foul, which, whether sweet or foul, are only of a day, and die. But one great love, and only one, may be to man who stands large natured and with powers too strong to die. Such love is central to him. Rooted in his soul it lives with it forever, and all the sweetness and the strength of him are in it as the sap is in the tree. So flower and fruit come from it, and such high ornament as make him glorious evermore. Such love did come to me, and in my soul I feel it growing more and more. One love I have, and only one. Another one I may not have, nor wish. It fills me as a cup is filled with water when its brim is wet. I drink of it, and, drinking the sweet draught, I thirst not, and I need no more."

And as he spake, yea, as the words were

on his lips, across the moon there grew a cloud, and darkened all the world. Black grew the sea, and heaving without cause from out the darkness came a moan, and a great wave rode in upon the darkness, and underneath the cliff broke with a fall that shook it; then, silence.

Then said Ungava, speaking softly in the gloom:

"Trapper, thy heart is fixed, and fixed too is my fate. Within the cave for seven days will I do solemn service. Then enter in, and thou shalt find him ready for the trail by which his body thou shalt bring to Mistassinni. There wilt thou find me by the cave that none may enter. There, with the mighty of his race and mine, shall he find sepulture. I would not change thy steadfast soul. It is enough for me as woman to have known thee and have loved. Thou art of ancient time. To word and bond, and nobler yet to love, living or dead, thy soul holds true. Long is the trail, but heart of truth makes tireless foot. Once more at Mistassinni we must meet. There shall we come to fate and its sad end. There shall we make last parting; and such parting will it be as never on this earth was made before! So fare thee well."

So said she, and then vanished. Then the cloud passed, the moon came forth, and on the crest of that high rock above the sleeping sea, he stood alone, while the white silence once more softly lay unoccupied on cliff and sea and shingled shore. And as he through the solemn silence slowly downward went he murmured to himself: "Die not, Ungava, lest from that cave in the Great Rock I shall come forth into an empty world. Alas! Alas! I would my feet might never tread the trail that leads to Mistassinni."

www.ingramcontent.com/pod-product-compliance
Lightning Source LLC
Chambersburg PA
CBHW050901130726
47900CB00015B/1577
9783337392284